The Wonderful Lamp

MAX VOEGELI

The Wonderful Lamp

TRANSLATED BY E. M. PRINCE

Illustrated by Felix Hoffmann

London
OXFORD UNIVERSITY
PRESS

Oxford University Press, Amen House, London E.C.4

GLASGOW NEW YORK TORONTO MELBOURNE WELLINGTON
BOMBAY CALCUTTA MADRAS KARACHI LAHORE DACCA
CAPE TOWN SALISBURY NAIROBI IBADAN ACCRA
KUALA LUMPUR HONG KONG

First published 1952 under the title of
Die Wunderbare Lampe by Verlag H. R. Sauerlander & Co.
Aarau Frankfurt am Main

First published in England 1955
Reprinted 1957
Reprinted in this edition 1963

Printed in Great Britain by Richard Clay & Co. Ltd.,
Bungay, Suffolk.

Kismet apportions
Food and Drink,
Life and Death—
The Gifts of Allah!

◆ ◆

ONE autumn morning I was woken up by the rain beating on my window-pane. Under a grey sky the countryside looked drab in the pale morning light, and as I looked out at the dripping trees and bushes I saw an old dog trotting up the road. There was also a man walking across the fields with his back bent down under the weight of the sack he was carrying.

I felt as if I had lost something and could not find it again. A dream of the previous night recurred to me—a curious dream—something to do with a magic lamp.

Ah! how depressing is wet weather! How boring when it pours with rain all day! Like someone with a pencil shading in a drawing for hours at a time. No doubt the best time to think out a colourful story. And so it was I made up a story, full of colour and movement, after the dog with his wet coat and the man in the fields had disappeared.

Bagdad—I thought—the Bagdad of Haroun al-Raschid with its legends and adventures. A thousand and one Arabian nights and a few more in addition!

And so, my friends, hear my story or let it pass. Allah (may he be praised) give you sweet dates and a green silken carpet from Peshawar!

M.V.

The Shah has the Pomp,
The Power and the Glory,
The Merchant has Gold,
The Wise Man Wit,
But the Beggar has only
The Crust he gnaws.

✦ ✦

HE FLED. He ran as only a street urchin can run. Stray dogs howled and tucked their tails between their legs. Pigeons fluttered in the air; he dashed by them so quickly that their wings scraped his forehead.

It was Ali, the beggar. Ali, the little nimble-fingered thief. He possessed the fleetest feet in Bagdad. And now he had to make use of them.

He had stolen a pancake in the bazaar. Now they were all after him: Chodar, the baker, Mahmud, the Turk, and Hassan, the eldest son of a potter; also a band of pickpockets and idlers who were for ever lounging around the market.

High into the air roared the cry:

'Stop thief! Stop thief!'

Down in the street swirled a knot of shrieking louts and cursing men: white turbans, red turbans and green trousers, amongst them the shaven heads of skinny beggars who cried the loudest:

'Stop thief! Stop thief!'

The street behind the screaming crowd was left empty,

except for abandoned objects: a yellow shoe, the red fez from a Turkish head, a green slipper ten paces farther off and, at the next corner, a blue cloth with an embroidered hem.

If they caught him, then next day there would be a fine show in the market-place in front of the white palace. The black-clothed officers of justice would drag him through the dust before all eyes. The executioner, all in red, would carry his axe on his shoulder; for any thief, caught in the act in Bagdad, must have his right hand chopped off. This was Djaffah's decree. Djaffah—they called him Sun of the Universe, Djaffah, the friend and adviser of the Caliph!

Ali knew exactly what was in store for him. He felt, however, no desire at all to give his right hand for a pan-cake—just one pancake, which was burning his fingers whilst he ran. He had done it the moment Chodah, the baker, was talking to a yellow Chinese girl. It had served the old man right. What did he want to tease a Chinese girl for in Bagdad! And with these thoughts Ali jumped over a street-cur which snapped at his heels.

2

At the end of the narrow street Ali dived to the left, out of sight of his pursuers. One moment they were looking at the bright red cloth he wore round his loins; the next, it had disappeared round the corner like a red poppy thrown away.

He ran with the fleetest feet in all Bagdad. Now he could no longer hear his pursuers' cries, so great was his lead. He panted and acted like a hare with the hounds after it. He turned right out of the second street and left out of the third, his black hair streaming behind him like a pennant.

Ali knew Bagdad. He knew where the narrowest streets and the darkest corners were to be found. He would soon be able to get his breath again. He was looking forward to enjoying his stolen property in peace. A tasty morsel! He carried the flat cake rolled up in his hand. The smell of hot fat tickled his nose.

He fell into a trot. Here the walls were so close together that they scraped his elbows. Suddenly he ducked, slipped through a hole with crumbling edges and—at last, here was peace. Here he could have his meal. Chodah had bestrewn the cake with white sugar. Ali sniffed at it; his mouth watered.

But he did not get so far as to taste his booty. Through the hole in the wall a boy's round head appeared. He could see a thin body, two skinny shoulders, naked and dirty—a pair of hands.

Ali had just time to make a quick bound. His heel, hard as leather from running barefoot, struck the approaching enemy and threw him back through the hole. On the other side of the wall there was a sharp cry of pain.

The little thief grinned at the sound. He crouched down beside the crumbling hole. A stone flew by and fell with a thud at the end of the narrow courtyard.

Ali laughed, and jeered at the bad shot.

'Thief!' cried his enemy. 'Thief—give up the cake!'

'Are you hungry, friend Hassan?' asked Ali as he bit into the pancake.

'Thief—son of a thief!' came the angry reply.

'You should be more polite!' said Ali and began to smack his lips noisily.

A second stone whistled through the hole and rolled along the dry clay floor. Ali was nearly doubled up with unholy joy. He had noticed how the lad was dancing up and down in front of the hole.

'Thief! You stole it!' abused Hassan. 'I saw you! You stole it from Chodar in our bazaar!'

'You are right, Hassan!' mocked Ali. He sunk two rows of sound teeth in the pancake, making shameless noises as he did so.

Hassan was the eldest son of a potter who had his workplace at the south end of the bazaar. Hassan and Ali knew one another well but they had never been friends. Hassan despised the little beggar with the red loin-cloth; as the son of an honest workman, he felt himself of better class. Moreover, he was taller and stronger than the little brown-skinned thief. But here Ali held the more favourable position; he was protected by the wall and Hassan did not dare to creep through the hole again. So he confined himself to all kinds of threats.

'I am going to call the others, thief! Give me a share or I shall call. Do you hear, son of a thief?'

Ali nearly choked with laughing.

'Give me a piece of cake or I will call them all. Do you hear? They will catch you and drag you to the market-place. They will beat you! They will give you to Djaffah's soldiers. Do you hear?'

'I hear,' said Ali with mock friendliness. 'Go on, friend Hassan!'

'I tell you again,' threatened the lad through the wall, 'give me some—or——'

'Too late,' said Ali with his mouth full. 'I've started on the second half. You came too late, my friend.'

'Give me what is left,' answered a greedy voice.

Ali laughed, munched and kept his eyes open, his foot near the wall ready to kick out with his heel.

'We shall beat you black and blue if you ever come to the bazaar again,' promised Hassan. At this he threw in a stone as big as his fist.

'Who are we?' asked Ali grandly.

'I and my friends,' shouted Hassan.

Ali could hear his enemy again approaching the hole. He said disdainfully: 'You and your friends! You're crazy—you and the whole gang!' He glanced quickly at the hole but it was only another stone. Then he popped the last piece of cake in his mouth and gurgled: 'Lovely and sweet, that was! Chodah covered it with thick sugar——'

'Thief! Thief!' cried Hassan from the other side. And: 'Stop thief!' He danced about with anger. 'Here is the thief!' But no one came into this narrow street where there were no windows in the walls; and his cries died out as in a cellar.

Ali laughed and coughed. He looked up and blinked. There, high up above him, a strip of sky could be seen, a patch of the fiercely bright midday sky.

'Here is the thief!' howled Hassan all the time. 'It is Ali! His grandmother begs at the Gate of the Prophet!'

It was only the pure truth that Hassan cried out to the silent street, but nevertheless it made Ali angry. It hit home: his grandmother was a beggar-woman. And Hassan screamed and raged so that Ali was afraid someone might hear him. Then, who could say, someone might seize the old woman and punish her for her grandson's theft.

'She begs at the Gate of the Prophet!' howled the lad through the hole in the wall. Then he had to stop to get his breath: this was Ali's opportunity.

'Your father fished mud from the Tigris:
From this he made a pitcher
Which was broken by Gulnar the witch——'

It was nothing more than a bad verse which Ali, crouching by the wall, sang through the hole. But it silenced Hassan and Ali knew why.

6

The little thief was famous for making fun of the street-folk of Bagdad. Many a worthy merchant had been annoyed by verses, made up on the spur of the moment by Ali and passed on, until every idler and good-for-nothing could sing them by heart. And therefore Hassan was now afraid of the rude verse being heard and repeated by others. So he contented himself with shouting some more abuse and promises of vengeance, and then took himself off, covering his retreat with curses and insults.

Once Hassan's cries had died out in the street, Ali grinned, very satisfied with himself. He cleaned each finger in turn on his red loin-cloth, slipped across the deserted courtyard, climbed up on to the wall and dropped down on the other side into a dark alley. And as he sauntered lazily past the closed doors he licked in the remaining crumbs of sugar round his mouth and began again his sing-song:

'His father fished mud from the Tigris——'

Grinning, he decided to polish up the poem; he was sure it would then be a great success.

In the meantime the narrow alley had led into a long street, sunk deep in shadow, at the end of which flickered sunlight.

Ali stopped and listened, blinking at the light.

He could hear the tinkling of little bells. Now he could see a camel over there swaying in the sunlight. A second camel followed and then others, camel after camel after camel, each one laden with a bundle; and amongst them black-bearded men, very lean fellows. They were wrapped in flowing garments and carried short lances in their hands. They were shouting in a foreign language, their shrill voices resounding in the street like vulture-cries. Ali began to run. He wanted to see some more of this caravan. He asked himself where they could have come from: from the steppes or from the desert.

When he came near he saw that both men and animals were covered with a rusty-red powder; the camels always brought that in the wool when they came to Bagdad from the east, out of the mountains.

The lad sniffed at the acrid smell of camel. To Ali's nose that was an exciting smell, giving promise of strange stories; stories told by the caravan leaders as they sat in a circle around the fire down by the Tigris. Many a night had the small beggar spent with these dark-skinned travellers. He had often begged one of them to take him with them—out of the swarming town—on a journey over the rivers into the far-away land of Yemen, to the Hedjaz and farther on to Jerusalem or even Damascus. They always laughed at him and sometimes teased him. When he became a nuisance they drove him from the fire with blows.

Full of enthusiasm, Ali went among them in the market-place, but he did not get far. Amidst a torrent of cries and clouds of dust the caravan halted. The little beggar was pressed against a wall by a shying camel. The animal pulled on his rope, snapping left and right, a dirty foam flying from its lower lip. Its burden, a heavy bundle of raw cloth, slipped down and hung threateningly over Ali's head. He made himself as small as possible but a sudden movement of the prancing animal knocked him down.

A driver sprang forward, cursing. The camel gave way to his blows and Ali jumped up out of the dust. His glance encountered a pair of black eyes.

Close to the wall stood a Negro slave girl. She carried a little yellow basket. Her broad mouth was spread in a grin and her white teeth shone dazzlingly in her black face. She

8

also had been avoiding the kicking animal; she now glanced at the boy's shoulder, which was bleeding from a scratch.

In her look Ali could read a passing pity. He made the most of it and stretched out his arm. Her black fingers searched in her basket and dropped a date and a few olives into his begging hand.

Then the rascal gave a laugh and said tenderly: 'Little black sister, you are kinder and more beautiful than the new moon which cannot be seen at night.'

The girl giggled and slipped away.

Behind the last camel came two men, talking and waving their arms about. Their caftans were made of brown wool. Ali could see that they were Jews; they wore the yellow strip of cloth fastened to their shoulders which Christians and Jews had to wear in Bagdad. They had very long beards, one brown and the other silver, beautifully waved. A broad-shouldered young man followed them barefoot. His skin was just as brown as the little beggar's. A ragged green cloth flapped around his head whilst his trousers were bright-blue, worn and much darned.

Ali skipped up to this man, who laughingly cried:

'Ho! little friend, light of my eyes, I was looking for you!'

'Give me water—only three drops!' begged Ali, fidgeting.

The young man was a water-carrier. With a jerk he brought round the inflated goatskin which he carried on his back, seized the end and poured a sparkling stream into Ali's sticky hands.

The lad smacked his lips, took a breath and drank again, his black hair falling over his ears and fingers. 'Some more, generous friend—more water!' he gasped greedily.

'Your thirst,' said the water-carrier, 'is greater than my skin!'

'I ran a long way,' explained Ali, 'that's the reason. And I ate something rich and sweet. It has made me thirsty.'

The water-carrier laughed: 'Was it something baked by Chodah, the baker, by any chance?'

'It was a pancake,' admitted Ali, grinning, 'covered with sugar as thick as your finger. Give me another drink, friend Zainab.'

The stream of water glistened in the sunlight and bubbled into the beggar's cupped hands. Ali sipped it with relish and sprinkled what was left over his face. 'That was help in the nick of time,' he panted with enjoyment. 'I was almost dying of thirst.'

'Come,' said the water-carrier; he gave the little thief a push and looked down on the market-place.

Over the top of a hundred moving heads Ali could see two black turbans. 'Djaffah's horsemen are everywhere,' he said and blinked. He followed his benefactor round the corner of a house. When they reached a niche in the wall, deep in the shadows, the water-carrier stopped and said softly:

'Little friend, light of my eyes! Listen carefully——'

'Make it short!' interrupted Ali. Uneasy, he looked through the low archway and saw the horsemen coming nearer: black horses heads with black coverings, and two spear-heads, shining in the light of midday.

'Come to this archway at midnight,' said the water-carrier. 'I will wait for you.'

'Alone?' asked Ali without taking his eye off the black riders. They were now so close to their hiding-place that you could hear their rough voices.

'There will be some men with me,' whispered the water-carrier. 'We have need of your talents, little friend——'

'I will come at midnight,' Ali whispered back.

'Now I must go——'

'Yes, yes,' whispered the young thief breathlessly. He pressed himself right into the niche, for he had noticed one of the horses turning and the rider looking straight at them.

The water-carrier put his left arm round his water-skin and stepped out of the shadow into the sunlight without a qualm.

There was a clatter of horses' hooves.

After a step or two the young man stopped and called softly:

'They have gone, little friend!'

'I saw them,' was the answer.

'They aren't looking for pancake-thieves!' The water-carrier laughed, his white teeth gleaming below his curling moustache whilst the green head-cloth tumbled over his eyes.

'Who knows whom Djaffah's horsemen are looking for?' answered Ali. It was a common saying in Bagdad. He blinked in the sunshine and ran his fingers through his thick black hair.

II

In the Desert live Djinns,
They ride hedgehogs and spiders.
Elves, ghouls and goblins
All obey the same Master.
And in the Bazaar
You'll hear what these are:
And of Wolf and Vampire
And the Magic Lamp's fire:
The story-teller rambles on:
He knows the seal of Solomon.

✦ ✦

'LISTEN to the story!'
Ali squeezed through the crowd pressing forward: scraggy Bedouins; yellow-skinned Turks with fat paunches; aristocratic Persians with pale faces and the street-folk in dirty rags.

'Listen to the story!'

Ali had been hoping for a good place but all he could see were the broad backs of the men in front of him.

'Hear the story of Aladdin!'

The story-teller was invisible to the little beggar-boy, but from the voice he recognized Mustafa, who was preparing to tell the people in the market-place the story of Aladdin. Mustafa! The best story-teller in Bagdad!

'Once upon a time in China there lived a tailor——'

Ali fidgeted; he wished he could see. Mustafa had a manner of introducing his stories with a mysterious waving of hands.

13

'—— he was poor. He had a wife. And his son's name was Aladdin——'

The voice of the narrator was now calm and his words flowed smoothly over the heads of his audience. Ah! Mustafa was an experienced artist who understood his art marvellously. Monotonously his voice rose and fell. Every word was distinct. And, like every oriental story-teller in the old days, he carefully guarded against over-emphasis.

Gradually the people in the street began to crouch down. At last the two broad backs which had barred Ali's view also squatted on the ground. Now he could see the story-teller.

Mustafa sat on a red carpet in front of a whitewashed wall, facing the semi-circle of silent listeners. At the specially impressive places in the story a murmur ran through them and the heads swayed to and fro. Mustafa raised his dark arms and his voice rang out louder than before.

'When the widow saw that her son Aladdin——'

The tailor must have died, thought Ali, shaking his hair. I must have missed that!

'One day a stranger came and asked Aladdin——'

The little beggar crouched in the dust, listening with only half an ear to what Mustafa was saying. While the story ran on Ali was inspecting the two backs before him. As already explained, they were broad. Over one of them was a yellow jacket of expensive material. The other back was wrapped in a rusty-red cloak. And it was just this rusty-red cloak that distracted Ali from the story-teller's voice.

On the right-hand side of this rusty-red cloak there was, in fact, a slit, through which you could reach. As the fat gentleman leant forward to listen to the story of Aladdin the slit widened and Ali could see into it. What he saw

14

under the rusty-red cloak held him more than what was happening to Aladdin in far-distant China. First there was a piece of dark-brown leather, part of the belt the fat gentleman wore round his middle. Then one could see the gleam of silver—a whole half-moon of silver.

It was nothing less than the round rim of a dirham.

'——the stranger was a wizard who had travelled from Africa to China. He said to Aladdin: "In this cave I will show you some marvellous things, my son!" He clapped his hands and the flames leaped up——'

Old Mustafa really was an artist! One of the most eminent story-tellers of Bagdad! As he described what happened when the African wizard conjured up a fire before Aladdin's eyes, his audience quivered with astonishment. They cried 'Ah!' and they cried 'Oh!' They wagged their heads. The fat man in the rusty-red cloak wagged his head particularly violently. That was why he did not notice the nimble hand reaching through the slit in his cloak.

'Aladdin jumped into the cave and went down the steps——' said Mustafa, raising his hand in a solemn manner and then letting it fall.

Ali bent forward.

'He found everything in the cave exactly as the African wizard had told him——' went on Mustafa, his right hand beating time with his words.

Ali bent forward once more. Mustafa's sing-song in his ears, he gazed at the gaping opening in the rusty-red cloak and the leather of the belt. He asked himself how many silver dirhams such a fine gentleman would carry around with him.

'Aladdin now sat in the dark cave,' continued Mustafa. 'In vain he cried out for help. He wrung his hands, all to no avail. But by accident he rubbed the copper lamp which he was to have brought out of the cave to the wizard. Suddenly there was a flash of lightning followed by a clap of thunder. Then out of a black cloud a spirit arose before him.'

Ali shuddered. He listened, entranced, whilst Mustafa lowered his voice and said: 'What does thou command, lord? I am thy slave!'

Ali bowed his head. A spirit like that, he thought to himself, that would be a fine thing! A spirit like that could make you rich. No need to go hungry any longer. No further need to fish round coins out of strangers' belts.

The little thief started; gooseflesh crept over his brown back. The fat man was putting his right hand through the slit in his cloak. Ali could clearly see his fingers feeling the belt under the rusty-red stuff.

'Aladdin answered the Spirit of the Cave thus: "Help me to get out of here if it is in your power!" And he hardly had spoken these words——'

Ali was no longer listening to what Mustafa was saying. He turned his head first to one side and then to the other. Men crouched in front of him; behind him also sat bearded men. The little thief saw that he was surrounded on all sides, as in the mosque. He would never be able to escape from this crowd. If the fat Turk should discover that his belt was lighter by one dirham . . .

In front of the semi-circle Mustafa went on with his story. 'Scarcely had Aladdin's mother rubbed the lamp with sand . . .' he was saying.

If the theft should be discovered, thought Ali, here I am like a rat in a trap. Anxiously he gave a quick glance at the slit and—oh!—the Turk had withdrawn his hand. His plump fingers were drumming on his right knee whilst, lost in himself, he listened to the words of the story-teller.

Ali drew a deep breath. He had been a hair's breadth from being caught. Then he noticed the rings sparkling on the Turk's fingers. There was one particularly fine one; a green stone mounted in silver. Ali wondered how much Harim, the silversmith, would pay for this ring.

Meanwhile the story was coming to an end. Mustafa was saying:

'Aladdin was free. The African wizard lay dead on the carpet. A few years later the white-haired Sultan also died. As he had no male descendants, the Princess succeeded him and she shared the throne of that great empire with Aladdin. And Aladdin's mother, who had once been so poor, became the grandmother of beautiful princes and lovely princesses, who played about her knees.'

The old story-teller made a closing gesture with his hand and cried: 'Great is Allah!' Thereupon he bowed to the left and to the right and all around him answered: 'Allah is Great!'

Ali got up and pushed a way out of the semi-circle of listeners, who now stood chattering and laughing by the white wall. At the next street corner the little thief stopped and looked back. Old Mustafa hobbled amongst the crowd which was gradually dispersing. You could hear the clink of copper coins as they fell into his brass bowl; the story-teller was collecting payment for his stories. But Ali could not see the Turk in the rusty-red cloak, nor him in the yellow jacket.

Out of a side-street six donkeys came hurrying in his direction, each of them laden high with brushwood. On the leading animal, which had a little bell tinkling from its neck, sat a small man with a red beard, Ali Baba, the wood-merchant.

Ali gave a broad grin. Putting his finger between his loin-cloth and his stomach he could feel the stolen coin, the dirham! A fortune for a small beggar-boy! Today there would be dates for dessert, sweet dates and good bread from the baker. Not just salty gruel as usual!

He turned off the main street. It was already twilight. Humming a tune, he went on thinking about the silver dirham.

Soon, high above the roofs, the muezzin would call the people to prayer.

He remembered that at midnight he must meet the water-carrier under the arch near the market-place. What was it all about? Some job, that was clear! But what kind of a job? Oh, the black-haired beggar-boy was used to doing jobs for other people at the dead of night. Little jobs which it was wise to keep quiet about. Often they brought him a handful of copper coins.

Humming his song, he threaded his way through streets and alleys where the whitewash was peeling off the walls and the smell of poverty reached him through doors and narrow windows. Here and there light flickered from open lamps behind the wooden lattices.

Ali's grandmother lived in a cellar. Turning out of a little alley-way one reached the beggar-woman's abode through a hole in the wall. Inside was a worn-out carpet which had once been red. The lad pushed this dirty rag aside and showed himself.

The old woman raised her head. She sat, bent, in a corner, stirring something in an earthen bowl. Her work was lit by the light of a tiny flame, given out by a copper lamp, very dirty and full of dents. The wick smoked and the place stank of burning oil.

'Gruel!' said Ali disdainfully. The carpet swung into position behind him.

Shadows danced on the lime-covered wall whenever the old woman made a movement. Her toothless mouth gaped. 'Each one of us,' she said reproachfully, 'eats what Allah has given him.' She bent over her task again and once more her wooden spoon stirred the thick gruel.

Ali grinned. 'Allah has given me something better!' he said and squatted down beside his grandmother. Then, with two fingers, he held up the silver dirham to the light of the lamp. 'I am going to change this coin into dates and white bread.'

'You have been stealing!' retorted the old woman.

'A rich gentleman left this coin with me, grand-mother,' said Ali. Shamelessly he added, 'He was as fat as this . . .!'

Then, with a wave of the hand: 'He wore a rusty-red cloak of shiny silk.'

'And you stole this dirham from him,' completed the old woman. She stroked a pale strand of hair from her fore-head and went on stirring the gruel. 'One day they will cut off your right hand in the big square in front of Djaffah's palace.'

'If they catch me,' answered Ali insolently.

'The day your mother brought you to me, you thieving grandson,' answered the old woman, 'was a day of mis-fortune. Go and throw the stolen dirham into the Tigris. Bad luck will stick to it!'

'I shall hand it to Chodah, the baker,' answered Ali, grinning.

'Chodah from whom you stole a pancake today!' said the crouching woman. 'I was sitting in the shadow by the Gate of the Prophet whilst they were crying after you. I could hear it all. Bad luck clings to every finger of your hands, Ali!'

'Bazaar chatter!' said Ali. 'Chodah will bless me for this dirham,' he added. 'I shall bring back bread and dates. Just wait!' he got up.

'Take your bowl,' said the old woman and filled a wooden platter with the grey brew. 'Eat!'

'I don't want any of that stuff,' answered the young rascal, shaking himself like a wet dog.

Squatting in the corner, the old woman began to eat out of the earthen vessel.

'Grandmother!' said Ali, standing uncertainly at the exit. And as she only went on smacking her lips without saying anything, the little thief continued: 'This afternoon I heard Mustafa telling a story about a lamp—a wonderful lamp. Whoever has it can become rich in a moment; you only have to rub it with your finger and a Djinn appears——'

'Throw the stolen dirham into the river!' said the old woman gloomily. Her protruding chin wagged up and down.

'I am thy slave!' said Ali, bowing, and his big black eyes shone in the flickering light. 'That's what the Djinn will say: "I am thy slave!"' Dreamily closing his eyes he added: 'Whatever the spirit is commanded, he does it in a second—if you have the lamp.'

'Take the stolen coin away, thief! Misfortune sticks to your hands!' said his grandmother.

Ali ducked under the hanging rag and went out into the street.

Here it was already dark.

He did not, however, throw the stolen dirham into the Tigris as his grandmother had ordered him. Nor did he buy any dates with it. He went and sought out Mustafa, the old story-teller.

Ali found the haggard old man in an out-of-the-way corner of Bagdad, not far from the great mosque. He was sitting in a coffee-house and sipped an aromatic brew out of a tiny cup. A green bird perched on his shoulder, industriously picking threads out of the back of his soft shirt.

Ali bowed like a well brought-up child. He also laid

21

his right hand on his naked breast and said, with deep respect:

'Salaam!'

'When beggars start being polite,' said Mustafa, it is time to look out!' He set down the cup on a little round table, winked and said, 'Little friend, what do you want from me?'

'O my lord and master Mustafa.' Ali was almost breathless with reverence. 'A question—just one little tiny question I would like . . .'

The story-teller leant back against the brick pillar by which he was sitting, and nodded. 'Ask your question, little friend!'

Ali slid down on to the carpet and crossed his legs like a tailor. With both hands he brushed the black hair from his face, put on a serious expression and repeated: 'Only just one little question, O King of Story-tellers——'

'Speak!' interrupted the old Arab, picking up some crumbs of bread from the floor and stretching out a finger towards the green bird.

'O great Mustafa!' Ali said. 'Did a Djinn really appear when they rubbed the lamp?'

The old man nodded. 'Most certainly a Djinn appeared!'

'And he fulfilled every wish?' asked Ali.

'Every wish,' replied Mustafa importantly. He plucked at his beard, which hung from his chin like a ragged cloth.

'How wonderful!' said Ali.

'It was a magic lamp,' Mustafa reminded him. 'In China,' he added.

'Is that very far from Bagdad?' asked Ali.

'Very few people from Bagdad were ever in China!' answered Mustafa. 'Scarcely a handful from the whole of Saoud, little friend!'

'Who, then, brings the yellow slaves?' Ali wanted to know.

'Just these few people,' said Mustafa. 'Sindbad the sailor brings yellow slaves from China. And Omar, lord of the great caravan, who once every year crosses the passes into Hindustan——'

'Hindustan?' interrupted the little thief; the word sounded strange to his ears.

'Hindustan,' said Mustafa, 'is a country on the other side of the rugged mountains. But China is still farther away, much farther!' He nodded and said gently: 'Was that the question you wanted to put to me?'

'No, Master, no!' protested Ali. 'It was another question I wanted to ask—just a little question only, O Mustafa. But—do you think the wonderful lamp is still in far-distant China?'

Mustafa expressed doubt by moving his bony head from side to side. 'The lamp,' he said, 'the wonderful lamp, little friend, I don't know where it is. If I did know, what do you think I would do?'

'You wouldn't tell me,' Ali answered, grinning.

'I wouldn't tell you or anyone else,' nodded the old Arab, his scanty beard fluttering in the air. Then he added: 'Some say that the wonderful lamp was taken by a caravan to Hindustan and afterwards brought on to Persia. Others say it has been lost and lies in the desert covered with sand to the height of a man. I have also heard say that the King of Kings in Hindustan made a present of it to our Caliph, Haroun al-Raschid—the splendour of Allah be on him. But who can know?'

'Then the lamp is as good as lost,' murmured Ali, dejectedly.

The old man's face relaxed into a hundred wrinkles. He

chuckled and said: 'So it is, little friend, light of my eyes. Aladdin's wonderful lamp is as good as lost. Was *that* the question you were wanting to ask me?'

'O King of Story-tellers,' panted Ali, 'this was not the question I——'

'What is it then?' interrupted the old man. 'How is this question of yours? Let me hear it!' He once more passed a crumb up to the green bird on his shoulder.

Ali saw that Mustafa was getting impatient. Now the old man was highly respected throughout Bagdad. He had often told his stories at the palace. Courteously giving information like this to a beggar-boy was the purest condescension on his part.

'This, O Sun of Story-tellers!' said Ali. 'This is my question. What must *I* do to find the wonderful lamp?'

The green bird chirped by the old man's ear. Lines appeared at the corners of Mustafa's eyes. Cautiously, he said:

'Little friend, that is *your* question. *I*, alone, know the answer. Tell me, how much can you pay for it?'

'I have some money,' Ali nodded, fingering the edge of his red loin-cloth.

'How much?' asked Mustafa.

'Enough,' said Ali, 'to pay for the answer to such a tiny question.'

'Your question,' smiled Mustafa, 'it is certainly short but it isn't so little. And the answer I *could* give you isn't little either! With the help of my answer you would be able to find the magic lamp, my friend. Think what that means. For that reason the answer will cost you a whole dinar, you see.'

'I see,' said Ali, 'but I haven't got a whole dinar. I haven't even got half of one. I only have a silver dirham.'

He fished out the coin and exposed it to Mustafa on the palm of his hand.

'My word!' The old man winked. 'A real good silver dirham. That's a lot of money for a beggar to have.'

'It should be enough to pay for your answer,' suggested the young rascal.

The old Arab looked straight at him.

'The coin is a good one, that is true. A real silver dirham. Yet there is something the matter with it, little friend!'

Ali opened wide his eyes. Mustafa, showing the black stumps of his teeth, declared:

'The coin was stolen, you know, little friend!'

'Stolen?' gasped Ali.

Mustafa raised his bony hand in admonition.

'*You* know, little friend, light of my eyes, and *I* know. You stole the dirham from a Turk in a cloak whilst I was telling the story of the wonderful lamp.'

Then, softly, and quite unexpectedly, he stretched out a withered hand:

'Give me the dirham, little friend! I will, all the same, accept it in payment for my answer.'

Taken by surprise, Ali dropped the silver coin into the Arab's hand. Mustafa tucked it in his belt, which was decorated with tassels. He then said:

'Twelve silver dirhams make one gold dinar. You will have to drop another eleven such coins into my hand before you will hear *my* answer to *your* question. Now go and leave me alone!'

The green bird flapped its wings and chirped.

Ali got up from the carpet. He looked very disappointed. 'Eleven dirhams,' he stammered, 'eleven dirhams —Oh King of Story-tellers!—that's a lot of money for a beggar . . .'

'Remember, my answer can get you the magic lamp!' said Mustafa. He picked up the little cup between two fingers and took a sip at it. 'What are you waiting for, little friend?' he snapped.

'Where in the wide world,' said Ali, hanging his head, 'is the beggar who can pay a whole gold piece for just a few words?'

Old Mustafa chuckled. Stroking his bird's green neck, he said: 'There are some beggars, little friend, who, secretly, are as rich as many a prosperous merchant. What about Fadl, for example, Bagdad's Prince of Beggars!' Then, surprisingly harshly, he added: 'Go! Leave me in peace. Go!'

Ali turned to leave the coffee-house. He was upset and felt he had been cheated. 'How on earth can I possibly get hold of eleven dirhams in a reasonable time?' he asked himself. One does not often find oneself sitting behind careless Turks who lose silver from their belts.

Deep in these thoughts, he knocked into a low table near the entrance, where two grey-bearded old men were playing chess. As his brown legs sent the black and white pieces flying, the men got up cursing him, and they started to lay about him while other customers came to join them. Ali only just managed to slip out under the carpet hanging at the door to avoid a thorough thrashing.

A little later, still panting, he found a niche in a wall to hide in, deep in the shadows. He ran his fingers through his black hair and looked up at the sky. A huge full moon hung between the black minarets of the Omar Mosque. It was high time to find the archway where the water-carrier was probably already waiting for Ali.

III

A thief's hand is light as a feather;
And the foot of a thief is like down.

◆ ◆

ZAINAB stood at the corner of the wall as the little beggar turned into the dark alley.

'All alone?' asked Ali. 'This afternoon you mentioned other men.'

The water-carrier moved to one side and then Ali could see four black faces behind him, under the archway.

'Negro slaves?' he inquired, surprised. 'What does that mean, friend Zainab?' Then he noticed a fifth man, standing farther back in the shadows.

'That man,' explained the water-carrier, 'is servant in a very distinguished house. He is going to take you to his master.'

'But why the Negroes?' asked Ali suspiciously.

'They are there to carry you, little friend.' Zainab laughed softly.

'Carry?' breathed Ali in surprise.

In the meantime the strange servant had come up to them. He bowed and asked:

'Is this the thief?' and his beard tickled the lad's nose.

'It is he,' answered the water-carrier.

'Come on!' commanded the man with a beard, seizing Ali's arm in a firm grip.

Under the arch, near the wall, was a litter, covered with stuff like a tent. 'Is there a woman in there?' Ali wanted to know and, bending down, he peeped through the curtains.

It was in such litters that elegant ladies were carried about the streets. There was, however, no one in the tent.

'Get in,' said the water-carrier. 'The litter is to carry you in.'

'I have been cheated once already tonight,' said Ali, and pressed himself against the wall.

The bearded servant gave a laugh. He again seized the boy's arms and, bending them behind his back, said: 'Little thief, there is nothing to be frightened of. It is only that my master does not want you to be able to find your way back to his house. That is why I must tie your hands together.'

'Let me go!' hissed Ali. He fancied he had fallen into some trap. But Zainab said hastily:

'Be quiet, little friend. Let him tie your hands. Let them carry you in the litter. It won't take long. Think of the reward!'

Ali made up his mind he would demand eleven dirhams for all this and kept still whilst the bearded one bound a rope round his wrists. A cloth fell over his face and he felt the ends being knotted at the back of his neck. He was grasped by firm hands and put in the litter.

He then found himself swaying about and fell back on the cushions as the journey into the unknown began. The slaves seemed to Ali to be going very fast. It occurred to him that in this way he would not be able to count the number of paces they took. The litter rolled like a ship at sea.

The little thief made up his mind to ask for a whole dinar as, he said to himself, a gentleman who could send four slaves, a litter and a servant to fetch a beggar-boy to his house must be as rich as King Solomon. In the meantime the front of the litter tilted up and he realized that they were climbing some stairs. He tried to estimate the time they had taken but that was not possible. Too many thoughts had been passing through his head since they had bound his eyes.

He was aware of a light, evidently coming from a lamp above his head. He blinked as they took the cloth from his head. A hanging lamp glowed red; there was blue and bright-green glass in it as well. It hung from a silver chain. The beggar-boy was in a fine house.

Zainab, the water-carrier, had disappeared. The Negro slaves with their naked feet retired noiselessly. Ali stood alone in front of the black-bearded servant.

'My master is a mighty man in Bagdad, young thief!' said Blackbeard. 'I am now going to take you to a room where my master will speak to you. But you will not be able to see him.'

Ali nodded and thought: He's a very careful one.

'You must be very polite,' said Blackbeard. 'Don't ask any questions. You must not move unless I tell you to. Do you understand?'

'I understand,' said Ali importantly. He felt confident now. He thought he recognized the game that was being played here. In his bare feet he followed the servant over the fine, expensive, silken carpets covering a narrow passage.

And this was the game. In those days, in Bagdad, rich people sometimes called in little rogues, pickpockets or cutpurses to help them in some shady business that could not be done by the light of day.

Ali was now standing in a little room with the bearded servant behind him. On his left was a window-opening, draped with a black cloth so that no eye could see out into the night. To his right hung a carpet with a dark-red, white and yellow pattern. A few paces in front of him was a wooden screen, dividing the room into two. This screen was covered with hundreds of little figures, wild animals and fabulous creatures, palm-leaves and flowers, which an artist had carved out of the wood with a sharp knife. Between the figures were small holes and through these he was aware of a man, sitting on the other side. His face, however, was not recognizable, as that part of the room was in the dark, whilst a lamp hung over the young beggar's head.

Ali laid his hand on his naked breast and salaamed as respectfully as if the Caliph himself had been sitting behind the carved screen. And as he bowed he noticed that Blackbeard behind him held a dagger in his hand. He thought: How timid rich people seem to be! Then he heard a croaking voice.

'They tell me that you are a smart thief, little friend . . .'

Ah!—he's old as the hills, thought Ali.

'—hm—hm—a very smart thief, little friend, light of my eyes. What is your name? Who is your father? Hm—hm—you are very young still!'

'Lord!' said Ali, bowing again. 'I am old enough for this business. I am Ali, the beggar. My father is dead. I never knew him. I think he was also a beggar. My grandfather, lord, what could he have been but a beggar?' He gave a little smile and looked keenly through the carved figures which hid the old man.

There came a croaking laugh. 'Ali,' said the husky voice, with a chuckle, 'Ali, the thief, son of a thief, grandson of a beggar! You are just the one for me!'

Ali bowed for the third time. He kept silent and waited.

'Have you ever—' continued the croaking voice, '—ever heard of Abu Bekr, little friend?'

'He is a great man in Bagdad,' said Ali.

'That is the truth, little thief,' came the answer. The old man chuckled and asked: 'Do you know his house?'

'Every child in Bagdad knows the house of Abu Bekr on the Tigris!' said Ali.

Behind the wall there was a satisfied little cough. The

old man said: 'Now pay attention, little friend, pay great attention to my words.'

'I am listening, lord!' assured Ali, laying ten fingers on his brown chest.

'You must bring me,' said the invisible old man, 'a book from Abu Bekr's house. A book—do you know what that is, little friend, light of my eyes?'

'I know, lord!' assured Ali. His eyes were by now becoming accustomed to the half-light and he could see that the old gentleman wore a long beard. He could also see that the beard was dyed jet-black.

'A book from Abu Bekr's house,' crowed the voice, and the jet-black beard moved behind the wood-carvings. 'A very special book,' coughed the old man. 'The book—I know it well—is the one book of a hundred in Abu Bekr's house. Pay attention to what I say, little friend! The book is bound in leather, the leather of a wild-goat. It is big and heavy, perhaps too heavy for you, little thief!'

Ali said quickly:

'It won't be too heavy for me, lord.'

A chuckle came back. 'It is a *very* heavy book, little beggar!'

The old man went on chuckling, coughing or clearing his throat at every word. Ali thought he could see him rubbing his hands continually.

'It is the book in which the great Abu Bekr writes down all his secrets. He is a famous man of learning——'

'A great doctor and a master of magic, lord, so I have heard,' said Ali importantly.

'The book,' went on the croaking voice, 'will be too heavy to take away without anyone noticing it. If you find it so, count seventeen pages and cut out the eighteenth. One leaf out of that book . . .'

'The eighteenth page. I understand, lord!' said Ali. 'Does that page contain the secret you wish to own, lord?' He glanced over his shoulder and noticed that the bearded servant knit his brows.

'You were not to ask any questions, little beggar,' came from behind the wall.

'I will be silent,' said Ali humbly.

'The book,' went on the old man, 'is in a room in an ebony chest. This chest stands near a window. The window—it is small—looks out over the waters of the Tigris.'

'I am listening,' said Ali.

'This very night, little friend. This very night——' There followed a cough, a chuckle, and then the words:

'Tonight Abu Bekr is not in Bagdad. I happen to know it. He is staying with a friend, who is a hermit, in the mountains. Only a few watchmen and the women are in his house on the Tigris. You must hurry, little thief! The moon is now high but soon enough it will be morning. By the first rays of the sun I wish to see the leaf—either the page or the whole book.'

'The whole book or the eighteenth page,' said Ali. 'Most certainly, lord!' He grinned at the wooden screen.

'Your reward will be great, little thief!' cried the croaking voice.

'And what about the punishment if I don't get hold of the book or the page?' asked Ali.

An impatient little cough was audible; then:

'Little thief, remember that my arm is very long in Bagdad!'

Ali bowed at the carved screen. He said: 'All the same, O great and mighty lord, you cannot do without the help of a poor little beggar-boy.' Quickly he added:

'I have heard you. I obey. This very night.'

'Go, then!' croaked the broken voice of the old man.
The bearded servant seized the lad's arm, drawing him
out into the passage. Silently the Negro slaves reappeared,
six of them now in their baggy trousers, naked from the
waist up to their shaven crowns.

Once more they bandaged his eyes and bound his hands
so tightly that he could not free them. The litter swayed,
the slaves ran quickly and softly. Quite a time elapsed; he
could hear the noise of the streets gradually fading in the
distance. They passed along empty streets. He sniffed the
air and was aware of the nearness of water.

When they had taken the bandage from his eyes he
could see the Tigris. The water glimmered in the moonlight; in the distance a ship floated down the current
towards the sea. And as Ali turned about he saw the
wall of Abu Bekr's house, which came right down to the
water.

'It's up there,' whispered Blackbeard, pointing.

The little thief could see, above the wall, a whitewashed
surface, projecting over the water like a dove-cot. Then,
to one side, he discovered the little window he had been
told about. It was protected by a lattice; a *wooden* lattice.

'But I can only reach it from the Tigris,' said Ali, dis-
pirited.

Blackbeard nodded. 'There's a boat ready. Come!'

The Negroes picked up the litter again and followed the
servant a little way along the river-bank.

'A boat is no use,' said Ali as they carried him. 'The
window is high up. I need a pole to reach the ledge.'

'It is a sailing-boat with a high mast,' answered Blackbeard. 'We will let the current carry us down to the wall.
When you climb up we shall all put our weight on the
near side of the boat so that the mast will lean against the

34

wall. You should be able to tear down the lattice; it is only flimsy woodwork. If we should be discovered, little beggar, we shall row off down-stream. You would then have to jump into the river. Can you swim?'

'Like a fish!' grinned Ali. Standing by the bearded man, he could see the Negro slaves tugging at a boat. As the bow touched the stones he jumped in. Balancing himself, he looked up at the bare mast pointing at the night sky. 'And where, you servant of a rich man,' he said, 'where shall I meet you again if I have to jump out of the window?'

'Under the same archway on the following midnight,' replied Blackbeard. He then softly gave orders to the slaves to push off.

Everything went off exactly as arranged. The heavy boat, in the grip of the current, was brought alongside the wall of Abu Bekr's house. Ali swarmed like a monkey up the slippery mast. The seven men all leant on the right-hand side of the boat till it heeled over and the mast pointed straight at the little window.

Ali gripped the window-ledge and, taking his legs from the mast, let it slide from under him. For a moment he hung helplessly over the water and then began with some difficulty to pull himself up on to the ledge. The curved dagger which Blackbeard had given him got in his way, so he put it between his teeth. It certainly looked very dangerous as, rather like a young pirate, he clung there kicking, the moonlight reflecting shadows of his movements on the white wall.

There was a faint cracking as he pushed in the lattice; it was no more than a window decoration. Ali shoved his legs through the opening and felt at once a soft carpet under his naked feet.

He stood listening in the dark. But he could only hear the swirl of the water as it flowed by under the window and, in the distance, the vague noises of the town; otherwise—nothing. Within the house all seemed to be asleep.

Ali rubbed his hands together: he was shivering. A cool night breeze played about his back. Ah!—there was a light gleaming under a hanging curtain, a strip of light, no bigger than a knife-edge. At the sight of it the young thief held his breath, rigid with fear.

But nothing happened. At last Ali said to himself: Either there is no one in the next room or he is sleeping like a pig, otherwise he would have heard me break open the lattice. He listened: there was nothing to be heard so he started to search around the room.

It was as well the moon was shining this night for it was almost like daylight over the waters of the Tigris. But here, in this room, it was much too dark to see an ebony chest. So the lad groped about with his hands until they came in contact with a wooden box. Feeling it all over, he found that it was attached to the wall by a chain. He thought: The great and learned Abu Bekr is a very suspicious gentleman.

Underneath the heavy lid Ali's fingers closed on the book of which the wheezing old man behind the screen had spoken. It was very heavy and bound in leather. Moreover, it was made fast by two small chains. It was with great difficulty that he heaved it out of the chest and laid it flat on the floor. In doing so the chains clanked. He held his breath and listened. No one moved.

In the dark Ali counted seventeen pages. Taking the dagger from his mouth, he cut out the eighteenth. It was not easy to do this as the leaves of this book were of thick parchment.

With the cut-out piece in his hand he stepped up to the window, and, leaning out, he could see the Negroes and Blackbeard standing up in the boat. They were obviously having some difficulty in keeping the boat alongside.

The top of the mast was so close that Ali could easily have grasped it, but he did not do so as he had just noticed something. And this something was a knife which Blackbeard handed to one of the Negroes. He also saw how the slave tucked away the knife in his trousers as he went up to the mast.

I have got to climb down that mast, thought Ali. I shall need both hands for it. That Negro has hidden the knife. What does he want it for? If I come sliding down the mast, his thought continued, that fellow can make me cold and silent for ever. Then they will throw me in the Tigris; they will have the leaf and the old man will not have to pay me any reward! I shouldn't be able to tell anyone about it either. I'll play them a trick.

He crept up to the window-ledge and sat on it. He rolled up the piece of parchment and fastened it securely to his belt. Then, taking aim, he dropped the dagger from his outstretched arm into the boat, hilt first.

The weapon rattled on the floor-boards. The men scattered. At the same moment water spurted into the air.

Blackbeard ran with a curse to the side of the ship, but it was too late. The little thief had dived over his head into the Tigris. They rowed about and beat the water with their oars, splashing around in vain. The beggar-boy did not show himself again.

At last they turned the boat round and laboriously rowed upstream. They tied it up, got out and carried the litter away through the winding streets. They walked with hanging heads. Later, in the house of the croaking old man, there was a terrific scolding for the servant, who had let a beggar-boy make such a fool of him.

As soon as the seven men had disappeared, somebody in the water began to splutter and spit. The heavy boat swayed a little. Dripping, Ali climbed up on to the bank. He had jumped from the window over the ship into the Tigris; then, diving down deep and swimming under the water, he had seen the shadow of the boat above him. He then came to the surface in such a way that only his head, from the chin up, was out of the water, under cover of the flat rudder. He had heard the useless splashing about and could see the splashers in the moonlight. Finally, he had heard the bearded man say:

'Turn round and go back. The young dog is drowned.'

He gave a broad grin and trotted away under the shadows of the houses. He could feel the folded parchment against his skin. He was cold for, although the water had been warm enough, the night-air felt cool after his bathe.

And, as only little thieves can, he slipped lightly through the hole in the wall and laid himself down on his bed of rags, whilst his grandmother went on snoring in the darkness.

There was a crack in the wall near Ali's bed. Mice sometimes peeped out of it. One brick was loose in the crumbling mortar. He felt around and pushed the wet parchment into this crack. Then he turned over and went to sleep, wrapped in an old blanket given him some weeks ago by a camel-driver.

He slept and dreamed. But he did not dream of the old man with the croaking voice; he dreamed neither of the burglary of Abu Bekr's house nor of his dive into the Tigris. No! He dreamed of the magic lamp.

A Spirit appeared in his dream; the Djinn of the Lamp in person! A fine-looking old man he was, with a white beard and eyes shining like moonlight. 'What dost thou command, lord?' asked this Spirit. And the little beggar commanded . . .

Well, what Ali commanded the Spirit of the Lamp he did not remember when he opened his eyes. But he had a feeling, a curious feeling, that he, himself, was a rich and distinguished young man.

Of course he wasn't a rich and distinguished young man. He was Ali, the beggar. He was reminded of the fact as he bound the red cloth round his waist. It was still damp from the previous night. And hunger gnawed at his inside. He had slept so long that it was midday or even later. Then he remembered the parchment out of Abu Bekr's valuable book.

Now an ordinary beggar-boy would not have known quite what to do with this. He would either have left the stolen parchment in the crack in the wall or else perhaps taken it to Fadl; Fadl, Bagdad's Prince of Beggars. Fadl would have given him a few copper coins for it or perhaps only a kick.

However, Ali was not an ordinary beggar-boy. Also, he knew that the strong betrayed the weak; people in those days were so untrustworthy. So he stuck Abu Bekr's parchment under his belt and strolled through the streets.

First he went to a letter-writer's booth in the market-place. Then his eye sought out the high minaret of the Omar Mosque and, keeping in view this tall, slender column rising into the bright midday sky, he looked for a house, ornamented with a bay-window. A gnarled tamarisk-tree must grow quite close to it. When he had discovered the house with the bay-window and the tamarisk-tree he turned about and knocked at the door of the nearest house on the opposite side of the street.

A black-skinned doorkeeper let him in. Ali said he wanted to speak to the master of the house. The Negro grinned scornfully and shook his woolly head, but Ali said to him:

'Run quickly, black brother, and tell your master there is someone here who knows something about the eighteenth page!'

The slave went off and quickly returned. He led Ali through the long passage into that room with the carved screen. In a niche, on silken cushions, sat the old man with the croaking voice. He now wore a bright-red gown and his beard was dyed red with henna.

Ali bowed low, salaaming with fervour. He also bowed to the black-bearded servant who was sitting nearby.

The two men had been playing chess. Now they had completely forgotten the game; Ali could tell that. The old man's red beard trembled; he croaked:

'You must be in league with the Devil!'

'Not with the Devil,' answered Ali modestly, 'only with your careless servants, lord! When I came into this room yesterday, that window on your right hand, lord, was covered up; and you, lord, had ordered this so that I should not look out and recognize in which house and in which street I was. That was very clever. But the cloth had been hung carelessly and slipped whilst you were speaking to me, lord, last night! And I could see the bay-window of the house over there, and the tamarisk-tree in the moonlight, and not far off the high minaret of the Omar Mosque. These three things showed me the way here by day. It is thus I stand before you, lord!'

'Do you know,' wheezed the old man, rolling his angry

41

eyes under the thin eyebrows, 'do you know, son of a beggar, that you are here in my power? Look behind you!'

Ali glanced over his right shoulder. He gave a broad grin and said:

'Lord, those slaves of yours behind me which you have secretly called in—I know them well. They were also there when I paid a visit to Abu Bekr's house. Only they will not dare to touch a hair of my head, otherwise you won't get the leaf of the book you want so badly.'

The old man coughed with annoyance and nearly choked. Blackbeard had to thump his bent back. Then, with a croak, he said, scoldingly:

'You sly young dog! I will have you whipped and tortured! You are a devil!'

Ali bowed and said quietly:

'Lord, I have the page. The eighteenth page out of the wise Abu Bekr's book. It lies well hidden with a friend. If you kill me my friend will return it to Abu Bekr. He will wait for me until the evening prayer; if I have not returned by then he will go and tell Abu Bekr, the friend of the Caliph—the splendour of Allah be on him!—who has had him robbed. Even so. Give me the reward for my work— neat work it was, too, by Allah!—then you will get the leaf which is of such importance to you, mighty lord!'

The old man clenched his hands in anger. He gave a hoarse cry and even foamed at the mouth.

'But who, you young Satan, says that it is the page I require?'

'It is the eighteenth page out of that book in which the wise Abu Bekr writes his secrets.' Ali solemnly laid the palm of his hand on his naked breast. Then drawing a breath, he continued: 'On this page, lord—please listen to

43

me—on this page stands written a recipe against the com-
plaints and distresses of old age! Now, O most worthy
one, judge whether it is the right page or not!'

The old man turned red in the face with agitation,
almost as red as the silk of his gown. He coughed and,
spluttering with anger, asked:

'How could you read that?'

'I myself cannot read,' grinned Ali, 'but Mahmud, the
letter-writer in the eastern bazaar, can read. He is a
Persian and, like Persians, wise! He read it out to me. I owe
him a whole dinar for that. And now, lord, give me my
reward so that I can give you the leaf of the book I stole
for you at night.'

'A recipe,' coughed the old man, fidgeting in his excite-
ment with the broad sleeves of his gown, 'by Allah! It
must be the right recipe . . .'

'You must take,' said Ali, recalling the words which
Mahmud had read from the parchment, 'take honey,
ginger, bertram—vinegar and hellebore—and garlic—yes
—add garlic and cinnamon, also sparrows' tongues; and
the cinnamon must be from China; then red pepper. That
is all.'

The old man had listened with his body bent forward.
He now gasped for air and screeched:

'Yes, yes, Allah is great! That is the recipe. But the pre-
paration, little friend, light of my eyes! I must also know
the quantities. Cannot you remember them also, little
friend?'

'I know about them, lord,' grinned Ali, and then
added: 'Pay me the reward and send this Blackbeard along
with me. I will hand over the page of Abu Bekr's book to
him and you will then be able to read it all for yourself.'

'Once you have the reward you will run away,' coughed

44

the old man suspiciously. 'Just as you ran away last night.'

'Allah is great!' said Ali. 'I won't run away—or swim away.' He gave a broad grin. 'Let us do it in this manner. You, O lord, give the reward to your bearded servant. He comes with me whilst I run and fetch the parchment. At a certain corner of the street we shall then do the following. With his right hand he will give a dinar of silver and a dinar of gold; so much I demand for my work. The silver is for the letter-writer. And I shall, with my right hand, take the money and with my left hand give up the leaf out of Abu Bekr's book. Our hands will thus cross and there can be no cheating.'

'A silver dinar as well as a gold dinar!' croaked the miserly old man. 'That is a lot of money for a thief!'

'As you say, lord!' answered Ali, bowing so low that his black hair fell over his eyes.

'Good, then,' said the old man, pulling out a silk purse from the folds of his gown. Secretly he was very satisfied, as a few days previously Abu Bekr had demanded five hundred dinars for the recipe and he had strongly objected to paying so much for it. Now he was getting it for a mere nothing.

'Allah preserve you, kind lord!' said Ali. As the old man placed the coins in his servant's hand, he bowed very low and added: 'May Allah cause Abu Bekr's medicine to be effective!' The old miser sensed the derision in these words and motioned to the little beggar to leave him quickly.

Ali stopped in the street and said to the servant: 'Hold out the money; here is the parchment!'

He drew the page out of his red loin-cloth.

With crossed hands they exchanged money and parchment. No sooner had Ali felt the hard, round pieces in the palm of his hand than he dropped Abu Bekr's parchment and, turning, ran like the wind. As he ran he thought: If the old fellow had known that I had it in my belt he would have had me killed so as to pay nothing for it. He dashed round a corner into a shady street, saying to himself: 'The stingy, croaking old vulture!'

Ali's most pressing business was now to find Mustafa, the story-teller, somewhere amidst the confusion of the swarming bazaar. He wanted to give him the missing dirhams. He wanted at last to hear what he must do to find the lamp. The Magic Lamp—which fulfilled every wish if you just rubbed it with the palm of your hand!

IV

Whoe'er has the Lamp—
Whoe'er has the Lamp
Needs no favours to pray:
Him the Spirits obey,
Calling him 'Sire',
Fulfil his desire.

He will talk with the fish as they swim around
And will understand whither the winds are bound:
Will find glittering treasure under the ground
Be master of Space and Time:

With the old lamp,
The old copper lamp,
With the lamp of legend and rhyme!

✦ ✦

'HERE,' said Ali, 'O King of story-tellers, here is the rest of the money!' He dropped eleven pieces of silver, which he had got in exchange from a Jew in the market-place, into Mustafa's dark palm. 'Now give me the answer I asked you for.'

The green bird on the old man's shoulder ruffled his feathers and put his head on one side.

'What was your question, little friend?' asked Mustafa, distraught. He was busy tucking the money away under the dirty fringes of his belt.

'What must I do,' said Ali, 'to find the magic lamp— Aladdin's lamp, the one about which you told the story? This, most worthy one, was my question. You promised to give me a good answer. It will cost me a whole dinar. I have just given you eleven dirhams and I gave you one before. Now give me your answer, Greatest of all Story-tellers!' Ali spoke quickly and eagerly.

'Oh—yes——' Mustafa yawned. He was sitting in the shadow of an overhanging wall. He looked up thoughtfully at the hot midday sky. He then lowered his head and put on a mysterious expression. Ali squatted close to the green carpet on which he reclined. And, stretching out a bent forefinger, Mustafa said:

'Listen well, little friend! Pay great attention to my words!'

'That I will,' replied Ali, almost in a whisper.

'If you wish to find the magic lamp, little friend, light of my eyes . . .'

'Yes, yes—go on, master, I am listening,' urged Ali, for old Mustafa was, rather ominously, taking a long time about it. 'Go on. What must I do?'

'You must,' said Mustafa, slowly, '—look—everywhere: above and beneath—left and right—whether walking or resting—only in this manner is the lamp to be found.'

'By Allah!' cried Ali jumping up. 'You have cheated me, old man!' He hopped from one foot to the other as if he had been bitten by an insect. 'For this answer I gave you twelve dirhams——'

'Which you had stolen . . .' nodded the dark-skinned Arab.

'I only stole one dirham!' insisted the little thief.

But Mustafa made a sign with his bony hand and said:

'One coin you stole, little friend. The others you were given for thieving. I know. Abu Bekr's house was broken into last night——'

'Bazaar chatter!' said Ali.

'Bazaar chatter perhaps, little friend,' answered Mustafa. 'Looking into your face I can read that this chatter is the truth. Listen to me, young black-haired friend of my old age. Pay attention to what I say——'

'I don't want to hear anything more from you!' cried Ali furiously. 'You have cheated me, old man!' He turned away and was about to leave when Mustafa called after him:

'He who thieves will never find the magic lamp!'

Ali did not turn back. Hanging his head, he passed out along the street and at the next corner ran into a street-urchin. The latter, as soon as he recognized the red loin-cloth screamed:

'Thief! Stop thief! He stole from Chodah, the baker, yesterday. Stop thief!'

'Shut up, Hassan!' hissed the little beggar. 'Long legged fool! Or else I'll sing about what your father fished out of the Tigris. Everyone will hear . . .'

On this threat, the potter's son withdrew mumbling. But the brown-skinned beggar felt, none the less, uneasy.

He stopped in a side-alley and began to think it over. Mustafa, he said to himself, has cheated me shamefully. The knowing old fellow was only interested in the money. He is despicable. But— he bowed his head, ran his fingers through his hair and thought: But perhaps he was right after all. Perhaps no thief can ever find the magic lamp. Theft, he went on to himself, is not agreeable to Allah. Yes, perhaps only with Allah's help can one find the lamp. Then, with a wave of remorse, he set off and going up to Chodah, the baker, gave him the one dirham remaining out of his ill-gotten gains.

The plump pancake-baker was not a little surprised. He wanted to give Ali back a few copper coins, for a pancake in Bagdad in those days did not cost a whole dirham. The lad, however, waved them generously aside and so Chodah gave him a nice crisp cake instead.

Young beggars are always hungry. Ali stood and munched away whilst the fat baker showered a hundred friendly names on him. In the meantime Ali's thoughts were elsewhere; they were with the magic lamp and with the words of dark old Mustafa.

'No thief will ever find the magic lamp . . .' murmured Ali.

Chodah put his fat hand to his ear and asked:

'What are you saying, little friend of my heart?'

'Oh! Nothing,' replied Ali. 'I was thinking aloud.' He looked as if he had just awakened out of a deep sleep after a bad dream. 'A thousand thanks,' he said at last, 'Chodah, king of pancake-bakers!'

He trotted off along the street with his head hanging and his feet shuffling in the grey dust. I am, he was thinking, a thief. That is true; and the old man had said that a thief will never find the lamp. He gave it a lot of thought.

When he had reached the Tigris, he stopped again and stared at the water. The swirling river flowed past him. The bridge of boats creaked in the current. People were hurrying from the western bank to the eastern and from the eastern bank to the western. The little beggar paid no attention to the white robes and the coloured trousers moving along it. His only thought was that a thief could never find the lamp. At last, with a grimace, he said to himself:

If that is really true, then Mustafa's answer was by no

means too dear! In future I shall never steal again: not a handful of dust! I *must* find the lamp.

As Ali passed along the bank of the river, the scorching sunlight rebounded from the stone walls. His feet, up to the ankles, were grey with dust. He was hardly aware that he was making for Abu Bekr's house, that house into which, only a few hours earlier, he had crept like a thief. He was imagining what he would wish himself once he had found the lamp.

A white palace on the Tigris! Fine clothes for himself and also for his grandmother! Sweets every day and water, fresh, cool water! Servants—slaves from Africa, from China—and tawny camels: very fast camels from the Hedjaz with which he could make a journey to Hindustan; for the name of this far-distant land, Hindustan, was for ever sounding in his ears since Mustafa had spoken of it.

He had by now reached the wall surrounding Abu Bekr's house. He stopped, took another step or two and knocked on the wooden door with his clenched fist.

The hinges creaked; the door opened slightly. A long and pointed nose appeared with a thin moustache below it. A grumbling voice asked the beggar-boy what he wanted.

'I must—' said Ali, '—I want——' he swallowed. His throat was dry. He passed his dry tongue over his lips and said with determination:

'I want to see your master!'

'In this house,' said Longnose, 'in this fine house lives Abu Bekr, the wisest of the wise, the friend of the Caliph, whom Allah has blessed!'

'Yes, I know,' nodded Ali, 'and I want to speak to him.'

'You . . .?' came the mocking retort.

'Yes—I!' said Ali. 'There's no need to be so surprised, Brother Sharpnose!'

To this there was no answer. The door was slammed and a bolt was shot home. Then Ali cried:

'Run, Sharpnose, and tell your master a young beggar is here who knows something about the eighteenth page! Run quickly. I am waiting.'

Ali looked across at the water. The people were going backwards and forwards on the bridge of boats, wrapped in flowing robes and white cloaks. There were also two horsemen coming across in black turbans and black burnous, each with his lance erect. They both rode on black horses. All Djaffah's horsemen in Bagdad rode black horses. Yet before they reached the river-bank the door creaked for the third time and Ali slipped through the opening.

He followed the servant across the courtyard. His heart was beating wildly as, in the servant's wake, he stepped into a cool passage and then soon afterwards into a dimly-lit room. Sharpnose made a deep obeisance and said:

'Here is the beggar, lord!'

Ali salaamed. He felt his last ounce of courage desert him. Then, as the servant was leaving the room, he observed a very big, but extremely thin man, reclining on a dark-red divan. His beard reached to his knees; he must be very, very old.

The little beggar trembled like a sparrow held in one's hands. He fell on his knees, imagining it must be the Spirit of the Lamp he saw before him; so tall and yet so thin was the famous Abu Bekr. His eyes glittered in the half-light of this huge room and his deep voice rolled, as out of a barrel, when he said:

'Speak!'

Ali swallowed. A hoarse sound came from his throat. Then he bowed again, so deeply that his hair brushed the floor, and whispered brokenly:

'I stole—O Lord—a page—the eighteenth page!'

'You stole from my book—you?' said the great Abu Bekr, surprised.

'Yes,' breathed Ali, wriggling his shoulders. He thought: Tomorrow already Djaffah's horsemen will be dragging me through the streets. The executioner will cut off——

'Why?' asked the lean old man.

'I stole for a man——' Ali bit his lips. He had no wish to betray anyone. Abu Bekr, however, asked with a threatening voice:

'You stole for a man. Is he from Bagdad?'

Ali nodded so violently that his head struck the floor.

'Stand up, little beggar,' commanded Abu Bekr. And as Ali hesitatingly got up, he went on, his grey beard rising and falling:

'Do you know that I could hand you over to Djaffah's horsemen and to Djaffah's executioner?'

With hanging head, the lad answered: 'I know it, lord.'

'And yet you have come and confessed?' said the great Abu Bekr. He leant forward and laid his hands on his knees. 'That,' he continued, 'I do not understand. Tell me the reason.'

'I came,' answered Ali, 'because I am sorry—and because I intend never to steal anything again.' He hung his head with shame.

Then old Abu Bekr laughed out loud, with such a roar that the little beggar's teeth chattered.

'You stole from me last night and have now come here to tell me so?' he cried.

'Even so, O Most Mighty——' gasped Ali.

Abu Bekr asked further: 'And why, son of a beggar, do you not wish to be a thief any longer?'

'Because,' stammered Ali, '. . . because it is displeasing to Allah.' He looked at the ground.

'Is that the only reason?' asked Abu Bekr.

Ali hung his head. He noticed a smile beneath the white moustache. So, with a sigh, he said:

'No, not only that. I don't want to be a thief any more, lord, because I want to find the magic lamp, the wonderful lamp of Aladdin. That is the reason. A thief will never find it; at least that is what Mustafa, the story-teller says.'

'Most certainly!' nodded the old man from his magnificent divan. 'So it is. No thief will ever find anything wonderful in his life.' Then, in his booming voice, he went on: 'Why, then, did you come to me, my son?'

'I came,' gasped Ali, 'because you are the wisest man under Allah's flaming sun. I came to ask you what I must do to find the magic lamp that can fulfil my every wish.'

'Last night you stole from me,' said Abu Bekr, 'and to-day you ask me for the key to riches and power! You're an extraordinary lad, my young friend. Come here and sit down.'

Slowly, like a dog not quite sure of his master, Ali approached. He sat down cross-legged on a blue carpet in front of the wisest man in Bagdad. Abu Bekr raised his long and extremely lean hand and stroked the silken hair of the beggar-boy. Then he said:

'I do not know what you must do to find the lamp, black-haired friend of my old eyes. But I can promise you this: if you will come here again tonight at midnight, then we will search together for the wonderful lamp. But you must first tell me the name of the man for whom you tore the eighteenth page out of my book.'

Ali swallowed. He could feel the hard fingers on his skull and was surprised that they did not start to drum on it. He kept silent.

The beard moved as Abu Bekr began to speak again.

'Tell me his name, little friend. Then I will tell you everything that is in my book about Aladdin's lamp. If you don't tell me I shall call my servants. Where do you think they will take you?'

A goose-flesh crept over Ali's naked back. He said, in a subdued voice, 'Djaffah's horsemen are everywhere. I know it, mighty one.'

Then Abu Bekr, grasping his hair, bent back his head until he could look right into the young beggar's coal-black eyes, and said:

'You have guessed right, my son. What then was the name of the man for whom you stole?'

Under his grip, Ali trembled. At the sight of the stern old eyes the blood froze in his veins and he said:

'By Allah! I do not know him—I do not know his name. I only know where his house stands.'

'Well, then, my son,' said Abu Bekr, 'go and show my servant this man's house.' Shaking his bony head backwards and forwards, he added: 'Return at midnight, little friend, light of my eyes. Then you will hear more about the wonderful lamp.'

The beggar-boy prostrated himself before Abu Bekr and said, fervently, 'May Allah preserve you, lord!'

As he was walking through the streets beside the sharp-nosed servant Ali thought: Never again will I approach too close to the hand of this terrible old man, him whom they call Abu Bekr Mahomet Er-Rasi. He shook himself like a wet dog.

Ali pointed out the house of the croaking old man to Sharpnose.

After that, he asked himself, am I now a step nearer to the magic lamp? He shook his head. Not that I can see it, he said to himself out loud as he stopped and scratched his ears.

'I am,' he went on, 'the same beggar-boy as I was before!' Looking down at his naked feet he said sadly: 'All I possess is the yellow dust on my ankles.'

'We appear to be equally poor, you and I,' said a dark-skinned man who had halted near Ali.

The little beggar raised his head and looked the stranger in the face. His eyes were screwed up as was the case with those who came to Bagdad out of the desert.

'This,' said the stranger, 'is a terrible city. Ten thousand human beings and no hospitality!'

'It is known as the City of Happiness!' answered Ali.

The strange man now showed his white teeth under his thin moustache and said:

'I have come from the Yemen, from the cliffs overlooking the sea. I hoped to find wealth and glory in Bagdad. But I shall now leave these narrow streets and wander back to where the Bedouins keep their sheep. There in the desert I was poor, but here in this City of Happiness I must die of hunger.'

'There are many beggars in Bagdad,' said Ali, thinking his words would console the Bedouin. But he only laughed disdainfully and said:

'I am no beggar! I am a poet. I make up poems.'

Ali grinned. 'O stranger,' he said, 'there are not only beggars in Bagdad. There are also poets and hungry dogs. I too make up verses and beg. What of it?'

'I am a really great poet!' said the Bedouin looking hurt.
So Ali said:
'Let me hear one of your poems.'
The lean Bedouin nodded. But he started with an
introduction ten times longer than the short verse which he
finally produced. So vain were the poets in those days.
The poem went like this:

'Bagdad is a beautiful town for the rich,
But the poor are just wretched, oppressed:
Without rest I just wander through streets in a maze
Like the Koran in the house of a Christian——'

Ali beat time to the rhythm with his head and then said:
'By Allah! Your verse certainly tells the truth. Would you
like to hear a little song I have made up? It is not quite so
sad.'
The Bedouin answered: 'Show me the way to the
Tigris. Your little song won't be any good!'
They walked side by side in the shade. They had to
squeeze through the crowd, as it was by now evening, and
the people of Bagdad were coming out of their holes to
enjoy the cooler air after the heat of the day.
As they were turning a corner Ali asked: 'Do you per-
haps know anything about a magic lamp?'
'Magic lamp?' repeated the Bedouin, avoiding a
donkey-driver who was urging his animal forward with
blows and curses.
'I mean Aladdin's magic lamp,' the little beggar insisted.
'That wonderful lamp which can fulfil every wish ...'
The Bedouin stroked his moustache and said slowly:
'Magic! No, there is no such thing! So there can't be any
magic lamps, little beggar.'
And he calls himself a poet, thought Ali to himself. He

felt very disappointed. After a short time he stretched out an arm and pointed down the street. Beyond the shadows and the moving heads water could be seen gleaming in the twilight.

The Bedouin made off, crying: 'Let me see the river. The Tigris! It comes out of the mountains and flows down to the sea. It can take me away from this city inhabited by ten thousand fools!'

'Ten thousand fools,' growled Ali. 'At the present moment it looks as if there were ten thousand and one.'

The stranger sighed and said solemnly: 'This river flows swiftly. It is wise. It has no wish to stay in Bagdad. Do you see, little beggar? It is making for the blue sea. The smell of the water in my nostrils is sweet and reminds me of my home.'

'Home and sweetness,' grinned Ali. 'It stinks of rank rushes and dead fish. Farewell, great poet!'

The Bedouin stared at the brown current flowing lazily by.

Ali went off along the river-bank without looking back. He thought: This skinny stranger is a fool, but, all the same, his verse spoke the truth. Bagdad really is a wretched place for a beggar.

He began to feel very empty inside. It occurred to him that, with the help of the wonderful lamp he would soon satisfy his hunger. So Ali decided to return to Abu Bekr's house at midnight. However loud the old man might roar, even if his eyes bored through you and his mouth smiled threateningly under the white hair, he nevertheless knew where the magic lamp lay hidden!

And so it was that when the moon was high he knocked on the wooden door by the river. They let him in. And old Abu Bekr wasn't so terrible after all. On the contrary!

He was very friendly towards the brown-skinned beggar-boy. Sitting beneath the glow of a many-coloured light, he told the black-haired lad everything he had learnt from the secret writings about the lamp.

Abu Bekr said:

'Little friend, light of my eyes, I must confess that knowledge about the magic lamp is a very complicated business, full of subtlety and cunning. Only a few men know this art. Their names are: Abu Jusuf, Abu Ma'schar and Thabit Qurra. I know a little about it because today, after you had left me, I read the writings of the true brothers of Basra. Three things you must know if you would find the magic lamp. Listen carefully to my words. Firstly, the lamp is of copper, mined in Tus. Secondly, when the lamp is rubbed a Spirit appears. This Spirit comes from the Elements, but his form is an Arkan, consisting of Heat and Humidity. Thirdly, you must know, little friend of my old age, that the magic lamp lies hidden in a place on the island of Qalah. It must be so. For the sailors say that there are copper and other metals. Moreover, this island is very hot and very humid.'

This was what the learned Abu Bekr told the beggar-boy that night about the wonderful lamp. And in the early hours of the morning, Ali ran through the streets and laid himself down in the dark corner on his bed of rags, just before his toothless old grandmother woke up. He closed his eyes but could not sleep. Of all Abu Bekr's words he only understood one. This word was Qalah! Now he would have to find Qalah, the far-away island.

C

V

Since Allah's time, on that far strand
No ship, no foot had touched the sand;
There where the steep and barren cliffs
Arose, untouched by human hand.

Towering rocks in an empty sea;
To the eye nought else appeared to be;
Sea-birds alone, with shrilling cries
Flew happily.

But inland lies hidden a beautiful glade;
A garden which Allah himself had made:
Blossoms aglow like jasper or jade,
With grasses as soft as a maiden's hair,
And crystal brooks are running there
So sweet to sip from the hollow hand—

That is Qalah, the far-off land!

✦ ✦

'QALAH,' said Sindbad the Sailor, 'Qalah lies far away in the deep-blue sea. What makes you ask about this enchanted island, little friend?'

'Because the magic lamp is hidden there,' answered Ali.

Sindbad gave a great laugh. And the men who sat with him in the circle also laughed and slapped their thighs. Brown-skinned fellows they were; they wore blue trousers, bleached by wind and sea.

'How do you know that?' asked Sindbad, his teeth flashing in the sunlight.

'Abu Bekr told me,' said Ali.

'Abu Bekr?' Sindbad's face grew long with astonishment. He twirled his black moustache between thumb and forefinger and remarked with a serious air:

'If he said so, it must be true. No one in Bagdad knows so much as Abu Bekr. He is the wisest of the wise!'

'They say,' went on the lad, 'that you, Sindbad, know all the seas. All the seas where ships sail. Is it true?'

'All the seas,' nodded the lean sailor. 'And a few more too, which no keel other than mine has ploughed.'

'Then you know Qalah, the island!' cried Ali, hopping from one leg to the other.

'Qalah—' said Sindbad, '—Qalah—' he again twisted his moustache '—Qalah, that's another matter, little friend. Very few have seen Qalah with their own eyes. I too have seen the island, but once only. It lay on the horizon, with steep cliffs. Flocks of birds were circling the rocks. But a storm came up from the east and drove my ship back. For a whole night long it soaked my sails in its fury. When morning came nothing more could be seen of Qalah.'

'They say also that since then you have been searching for the island?' said Ali.

'It is so,' admitted the famous sea-captain.

'Take me with you in your ship!' cried Ali. 'Please, mighty Sindbad! Take me with you. I *must* find the magic lamp!'

'Did Abu Bekr really tell you that the lamp lies hidden on Qalah? Was that not a lie, little friend?' Bending forward, Sindbad looked straight into the boy's eyes.

'He said it, really and truly!' insisted Ali. 'He also said I must do all I can to find the island, really and truly!'

'In that case,' said Sindbad, 'you can come with me, little friend. If Abu Bekr says it, it must be so. For he knows a great deal. He knows even more than I. And

that—' added Sindbad, '—that is hardly to be believed! As a matter of fact I know the whole world and have been everywhere. He, on the other hand, has only been to Tus once, on a camel, and twice was he in Mecca.'

The sailors all nodded their agreement and, as one man, said: 'Allah is great!'

Thus it happened that Ali, the beggar-boy, sailed in a ship out into the wide world to look for Qalah, the island of Qalah, and the magic lamp which can fulfil every wish.

However, before he went on board the ship, he said farewell to his grandmother.

'Good-bye and do not be sad,' he said. 'When I come back we shall be as rich as King Solomon, you and I!'

The old woman who was eating her gruel, replied: 'I am content so long as you are with Sindbad. He is a great captain.'

'Yes,' nodded Ali, 'I must go . . .' But he did not go at once. He surveyed the narrow room which was little more than a cave. He thought: Many a year have I lived here. The light from the old copper lamp flickered and the wick smoked so badly that it brought tears to his eyes. Shadows danced on the cracked wall. The old woman sat hunched up and chewed with toothless gums. Ali swallowed and put a hand to his nose.

But the moment he had passed out into the street all was forgotten. He now thought only of the *Prince Omar*, as Sindbad the Sailor's famous ship was called. She lay moored in the harbour.

He ran through the streets and alleys down to the river. And as he saw in the moonlight the masts of many ships rocking sleepily on the water, he was overcome by a longing to travel, and his heart beat fast. It was now only a question of getting away from the City of Happiness; first to Basra and then on to the Persian Gulf.

For very joy Ali pressed his folded blanket against his naked breast. He could now see the slender bow of Sindbad's ship across the dark water. He ran towards it along the bank of the river. The *Prince Omar's* mast pointed up at the stars. A shadow appeared at the ship's side.

'Where are you going, lad?'

'On board!' cried Ali.

Twenty heart-beats later he was pulling with Sindbad's men on a thick rope. As he tugged away with panting breath, the round moon suddenly disappeared. And he

knew that they were hoisting the sail, hiding the stars from
him, hoisting it up the mast so that it could catch the wind.
At the same time he found the deck of the ship under his
feet sinking and then rising gently, beautifully gently, as

she felt the current under her; for she was now moving in the breeze. He could also see how, on the starboard side, a nimble shadow leaped about, holding a bar across his chest—that was the helmsman. Forward, the curved bow swept across the sleeping houses on the shore. Downstream the ship was borne by current and breeze towards Basra. And the beggar-boy, full of enthusiasm, danced about between coils of rope and water-skins. He laughed and laughed until Sindbad stumped up the ladder and said:

'You will wake up the river for us, little Djinn. Be quiet so that the men can sleep.'

Ali looked around him. Moonlight and curling shadows glided hither and thither. Wrapped in thick blankets, the sleeping sailors looked like lifeless bundles. Only the man at the helm and a lad up above still kept watch.

'He is the look-out,' said Ali to Sindbad. 'I, too, could do that.' He pointed with his thumb at the dangling legs on the cross-bar. 'And *he* is holding the rudder.'

Sindbad nodded and twirled his moustache.

'The Tigris is dead,' said Ali, peering into the wake the ship left behind, shining like molten lead. On either side the banks appeared like two dark lines between starlight and water.

'Ships seldom sail here at night,' said Sindbad. 'But I want to get to Basra quickly. We have a long way to go, an unknown way in a strange sea.'

'I wish we could see the island already,' grumbled Ali. He shivered a little. 'Qalah!' A gooseflesh crept over his back. The wind coming off the land was freshening. It filled out the triangular sail in such a fashion that it pulled at the braces and looked like a cloud, or a huge funnel, or some flying creature. Below, the shadow of the ship glided over the stream.

65

'You will have to dance for many days under this sail before you catch sight of Qalah,' said Sindbad.

Ali raised his head. The prophecy made no sense at all to him. The wiry seaman only laughed, showing his white teeth. He laid a hand on the boy's shoulder and said:

'Take your blanket, little friend, and—sleep! In the morning there will be work for you to do.'

Sindbad's long legs picked their way through the sleeping sailors and clanked down into the cabin. Ali undid his bundle and lay down where he was, on the deck. It is true that his blanket smelt rather of camel but it gave him warmth. He tucked it round him and lay with open eyes, listening to the gurgle of the wake and to the flotsam striking against the hull. Between the rigging and the cross-bar he could see the stars in the night-sky; only Allah could know what they were up to!

And so he slept, slept like a log and did not wake up until he heard the boards under his head resounding to dull thuds. In the east it was dawning. Sindbad's men were running about the deck, their naked feet making a noise like the beating of drums. Then, like a crowing cock, a sailor's head and neck appeared from below crying:

'Run and heave, you sons of the sea! Heave-o! The morning has come. The east wind is with us! Catch it, you cringing dogs! Catch this splendid wind!'

He roared so loudly that he turned red in the face as he beat time with his clenched fists on the wooden rail.

Ali threw aside his coarse covering. He leaped around, clinging to the rope's end at which Sindbad's sailors were hauling. They were shortening the sail that had hung all night over the water so that the morning breeze would strike the taut canvas in just the right place. Now the wind caught the tightened surface and drove the ship forward at a greater speed. The *Prince Omar*, with her beautiful slender lines, heeled over in the wind. The bow-waves foamed along the hull and were left behind as white flakes in the grey morning light. For the first time in his life, Ali understood, as he stood with Sindbad on the poop, how a sail could be made to run against the wind.

'This is the great semi-circle before Kut-l-Amara,' said the sailor, pointing with his arm at the eastern horizon where the Tigris made a big loop.

Ali blinked. A ball of fire was shooting up over the horizon. The lad closed his eyes. He could see only a blurred world of tongues of flame and dazzling water.

'Now it is day,' laughed Sindbad. 'Our day!' He smiled as he saw Ali holding his hands to his eyes. 'We are already a long way from Bagdad and half-way to the first shallows where a hundred thousand frogs are croaking. You will hear them, little friend.'

But before Ali came to hear the hundred thousand frogs he experienced a dreadful hour at the mast-head. The great Sindbad had said, once the sun had properly risen:

'Now little friend, up to the crow's-nest! You have got to become a real sailor. Keep your eyes open. Whatever you may see ahead of us you must report to the steersman.'

He was soon perched on the round cross-bar right under the fluttering pennant. The *Prince Omar* ran on an easterly course, straight into the climbing sun.

The mast bowed sideways deeper and deeper, rose again, dipped again, deeper than ever. And Ali rose and dipped with it. He looked ahead. Below him gleamed the shining Tigris and its curving banks. And, as if by witchcraft, now it was not the mast which rose and fell but the banks of the river to the right and to the left. The land behind them did the same, climbing up to the skies on one side and sinking down into the depths on the other, and then the reverse. The little beggar shut his eyes but it did not help him as he could now feel his very inside repeating the movement. And down below he could hear the captain's voice crying:

'Fetch the lad down from the mast. He's sea-sick!'

'Allah be praised!' groaned the boy as he grasped the mast. At that moment his legs slipped from their perch and dangled through the sail in the open air. It seemed an age before powerful hands seized him and lifted him down to the deck.

'Put him in the shade,' said Sindbad. His laugh rang out as he looked at Ali's pitiful face.

The little beggar did not open his eyes until the sun had sunk and night had fallen over the land and the gliding river. Then he crept from under the companion-way and, on all fours, crawled up to the water-skin fastened to the mast. He sipped a little water, but it was lukewarm and tasted sweet, turning up his stomach.

'That doesn't matter, little friend,' grinned Sindbad. 'The sooner you get it out of you the sooner you will be able to fill yourself with dates and gruel again.' As he said the word 'gruel' Ali groaned and, pressing his hands against his stomach, crept to the rail where he hung his head and shoulders overboard. In the dark he looked just like a bundle of wet rags someone had thrown down. And the sea-sick lad was lying in the same position at midnight when the frogs could be heard in the distance. He heard them all right, but the concert gave him no pleasure.

In the meantime the *Prince Omar* had reached the shallows where the river divides into narrow channels running between islands of sedge and rushes. Here the very air stank of rottenness. Ali suffered further pangs of sea-sickness and then, when the worst was over, he groped his way down the wooden ladder. With chattering teeth, he rolled himself in his old blanket. The acrid smell of the rough cloth consoled him a little because it reminded him of dry land. He pressed his fingers in his ears, for it seemed as if *two* hundred thousand frogs were croaking round the ship, filling the muddy swamp with their wretched sound.

The next day Sindbad, looking under the companion-way, said: 'Little friend, you are not only sea-sick but you have a fever.' He called a black-skinned member of the crew.

This sailor—they whispered that he knew something about witchcraft—rummaged in his clothes for a piece of tamarisk-rind as big as his hand. He scraped it with a knife and finally gave the boy a pinch of dust to swallow.

But it took a long time for the medicine to take effect. Days passed. The town of Obolla lay behind them and Ali did not see the meeting of the Tigris with his brother Euphrates there. The lad fevered and shivered and sweated all the time. The *Prince Omar* had sailed through the Hor al Hammar and at last arrived at Basra. There were here many ships in the harbour. One of these was so large and of such curious build that Sindbad's sailors hung chattering like inquisitive monkeys in the rigging. The famous Sindbad said that the ship must be from China. He also told them that the Chinese sailed with a good three hundred men on board; and when the crew would not believe him he laughed at them.

Ali of course believed what Sindbad said, but he could not see the Chinese ship, as he lay with chattering teeth under the ladder, wrapped in the hairy blanket. When, a little later, Sindbad brought him some fresh water to drink, he asked:

'Where are we? The waves under the ship are different. I can feel it.'

Pleased, the wiry Sindbad laughed and replied: 'My ship is passing through the Schatt al Arab, towards the open sea. What you feel is the tide in the Persian Gulf, meeting the current and set against us. You are going to make a splendid sailor, little friend!'

'I am going to die, great Sindbad,' said Ali, closing his eyes.

'You will go to sleep and be better again as soon as we get out to sea. Salt air drives away fever.'

70

Ali did not believe Sindbad's words. He went to sleep, nevertheless, and slept the whole day and a night until the following midday. When he woke up he at once felt much better. He crept out from his blanket and said:

'I am hungry.'

They gave him dates and water. He smacked his lips as he ate and spat the date-stones overboard to windward.

'What did I say yesterday?' asked Sindbad, standing on the poop and looking over his crossed arms at his new cabin-boy. 'You are well again, little friend! The salt sea air has done that. We are already far from Basra, very far from Bagdad—so many days nearer our island.'

'Qalah!' said Ali, spitting and watching the date-stones fall into a passing wave. 'Qalah and the magic lamp!' He swallowed and added: 'I had forgotten why I was in your ship, great Sindbad.'

The sailor laughed.

Ali let the sea-breeze ruffle his hair. His eye followed the waves which stretched from the ship's side to the horizon. The sky was as blue as blue. The sun was burning hot. And the taste of the dates was like honey on his tongue.

In the meantime they had sighted a small sail in the shimmering distance.

'That will be Captain Abass with his dhow on the way to Sohar. In the hold will be chained slaves: Moors, men and women—that's the cargo he deals in.'

At this moment the dark-skinned sailor who had scraped Ali's medicine from the tamarisk-rind stepped out from under the sail and said:

'Don't spit any more date-stones to windward, lad! That is dangerous!'

'Dangerous?' Ali gave a broad grin.

'Spirits follow every ship,' replied the sailor seriously, 'the Djinns of the sea!' He then murmured something unintelligible and rolled his eyes until you could see the whites of them. 'Whoever spits date-stones to windward could easily strike a Djinn on the head. That would sink the ship!'

'Which is windward?' asked Ali.

Up on the poop, Sindbad answered: 'Windward is the side the wind comes from. It disappears to leeward, little friend.'

The black-skinned sailor turned up his nose and shook his mop of hair with displeasure.

'And how,' asked Ali further, 'you wise man, do you know anything about these spirits? I can't see any, not a Djinn nor a ghoul! All I can see is water and waves and sky and the wind in the sail!'

'I know,' said the sailor crossly. 'You don't understand anything about it.'

'But I should like to know,' answered Ali quickly, for a sudden idea had occurred to him: perhaps he would know something about Aladdin's wonderful lamp. 'Gladly, O most wise one!'—he sighed—'Gladly would I learn of these things.'

'Come up to the poop at midnight,' said the dark one. 'I am on watch then and I will tell you.'

Ali was very pleased at the idea. He loved stories, especially ghost stories. Perhaps an important word or two about the magic lamp would be dropped. Who could know?

At midnight he sat with his blanket, feeling rather creepy, next to the sailor who was so black that he was only just visible in the starlight. In front of them the sail loomed like a huge cloud; the yard-arm creaked as it rubbed against the mast. The waves came from the north-east, white-crested, like fluttering birds appearing out of the night and beating against the hull. From time to time a high wave broke over the bow, showering the deck with water which shone in the moonlight.

'Witchcraft and sorcery,' said the black sailor, 'are learnt in Babylon. There the angels Harut and Marut are locked up in the old walls because they rejected the truth of Allah.'

Ali sat as still as a mouse, listening intently.

'But if you want to become a really great wizard, lad,' continued the Negro, 'then you must go to southern Arabia, to the chilly caves that are known as Haoud-Kovvir. They lie between solitary rocks. There you must sacrifice a black yearling kid at twilight. You must divide it into seven portions. Cover the entrails with the skin. At midnight you must carry the seven portions into Haoud-Kovvir. But there must be no human being within a circumference of one hour's walking.'

'What will happen then?' asked Ali.

'Have you got any great wish?' asked the sailor.

'Oh, yes,' said Ali emphatically, thinking of the magic lamp.

'Well,' went on his companion, 'you must lie down to sleep at midnight in Haoud-Kovvir, thinking hard of your great wish. But first you must rub yourself all over with the kid's blood.'

'Brr!' Ali shuddered.

'Yes, that is necessary,' continued the sailor. 'Then if you wake up in Haoud-Kovvir and find that your skin is as clean as if you had bathed, your wish will be fulfilled. Wherever you then may go, you will quickly get the thing you have wished for.'

Ali drew a deep breath and said: 'Praised be Allah! I

73

need never sleep in this dreadful cave. *My* wish will be fulfilled as soon as our ship is anchored off the shore of the island of Qalah.'

'You are thinking of the magic lamp, lad?' asked the sailor. Ali could see in the starlight how he craned his neck. He nodded. Then the Negro said:

'But supposing you don't find the lamp? Remember, it is a magic lamp, a ghost lamp! A Djinn may have taken it away from the island.'

'Then that will be time enough to make a pilgrimage to the horrible Haoud-Kovvir,' said Ali.

'Now, wait a minute, lad,' growled the sailor. 'It is not so easy as all that. Are your parents still alive?'

'Only my grandmother,' said Ali.

'There you are; then it's no good!' cried the sailor. 'Whoever has parents or grandparents living, he will never leave Haoud-Kovvir alive.'

'But why not?' Ali wanted to know.

'I must not tell you why; but it is so. Still there is no need to despair. Perhaps I can find a means whereby you can, nevertheless, sleep in the cave, so that your wish may be fulfilled. Tell me about yourself, lad.'

'There is not much to tell,' said Ali in a small voice. 'I lived with my grandmother in Bagdad before I came on board this ship. She once told me that my father had been a foreign ship's captain. He never returned to Basra where my mother used to live. That was why she wrapped me in some clothes and brought me to Bagdad. But she died soon after of the plague, before the gates of the City of Happiness. I was then five years old. I learnt to beg. When I grew bigger I also stole sometimes. Now I never steal—nothing whatever. Mustafa told me that a thief could never find the lamp. The wise Abu Bekr, the friend of our Caliph—

Allah's splendour be upon him!—he said the same thing. That is why I am now only a beggar searching for Aladdin's lamp.'

'Good,' said the black sailor. 'I know of a means to help you. You must swallow it. It is a potion of rare herbs. Then you will be able to sleep in Haoud-Kovvir without harm——'

'Provided the lamp is not on the island,' interrupted Ali.

'If the lamp has disappeared from the island,' nodded the Negro.

'And, O wise man!' cried Ali. 'What is the name of this drink and of the herbs in it which will help me to fulfil my wish?'

'Oho!' growled the sailor. 'Not so fast!' He stretched out his legs on the deck. 'I did not steal my knowledge; it cost me much labour and magic!' He leaned against the rail and asked: 'What will you give me if I obtain this magic potion for you?'

'What do you want?' asked Ali. He was reminded of the haggling with Mustafa in Bagdad.

'Sindbad—' said the black one, '—Sindbad, it is true, is looking on this journey for the island of Qalah. But he also wants to earn money. On the return voyage the *Prince Omar* will call at the far-away island of Ceylon. There we shall load coconuts. Every sailor in Sindbad's crew will be given a share of the cargo—you also, although you are only a useless lad.'

'What is it you want then for your magic potion?' asked Ali.

'Your share of the nuts,' said the sailor. 'It is a very costly potion; the herbs are very hard to find. But they are very powerful.' He stood up and gazed intently at the boy.

'Very costly and very powerful!' murmured Ali, getting

75

up from the deck. His face broke into a broad smile. 'When, O wise man, will you give me this potion?'

'As soon as I have sold your share of nuts in Basra,' answered the sailor graciously.

'No thank you,' answered Ali. 'Your story of the Haoud-Kovvir—that was good. But your magic potion—no! I was already cheated once in Bagdad by an old story-teller. You are a sailor, perhaps a wizard, my black friend, but all the same you are not going to cheat me.'

The fellow stood stock-still, as if glued to the deck. Then, suddenly, uttering a fierce oath, he went for the cabin-boy with both fists.

Ali ducked and, avoiding the blow, butted his opponent with his head violently in the midriff.

The magician staggered back against the rigging, doubled up and howling with pain. This woke the sailors on the deck below and they hurried to the scene. Sindbad, however, who had been standing in the shadow of the sail and who had heard everything, was the first to reach the poop. He stooped over the groaning wizard and said:

'That will teach you, my son. If you want to find someone to cheat, see that he doesn't come from Bagdad. Nowhere will you find such suspicious people as in Bagdad, although they may believe in magic lamps and enchanted islands. But they don't believe in costly magic potions!' He laughed loudly.

The next day Ali took care not to get within reach of the black man's feet or fists, as Sindbad had said to him:

'Take care, little friend, light of my eyes. The magician is furious. He will seize the first opportunity to throw you in the sea.'

'And if he misses that opportunity, great Sindbad?' Ali had asked.

'Then you won't have to join the fishes and will find the magic lamp,' Sindbad had said, and Ali had laughingly rejoined:

'I am not going to join the fishes!'

No, he did not fall overboard. On the contrary, every day he became a better cabin-boy and Sindbad promised him in consequence a share of the cargo which they were to load in Ceylon. The wizard was right about this.

Day after day the straining bow of the *Prince Omar* pointed southwards in that direction where, in the boundless blue sea, Qalah must lie. The heat increased. Evening after evening rose the stars before the little beggar's eyes— the southern stars, sparkling light-signals in the heavens— night after night. *They* pointed the way to the sailor. It was a wonderful voyage with a favourable wind, which Allah blew over the waters.

Of course it was a fine voyage! The ship was manned by a capable crew who were all good Muslims. If there was a wizard amongst them—what then? Every sailing-ship has her Jonah on board. Magicians and mountebanks, ghouls and spirits: there were plenty of them everywhere in Sindbad's time. Sometimes even the mischievous Shaitan himself visited mortals and played his jokes on them. What did it matter? They said a prayer and the devil put his tail between his legs and made off.

Five times a day the captain called them to prayer. He stood on the poop and led the muezzin for his crew. Oh, yes, the great Sindbad was a pious man. Using his hands as a megaphone, he roared:

'*Allahu akbar!*'

Sindbad shouted this simple sentence three times; for it means: 'Allah is great!' Then followed fairly quickly the words:

77

'. . . *Aschdu anna la illaha ill a-llah wa Muhammadun rasalu-llah' hajja ala-ssalah!'*

This means: 'I swear that there is no other God than Allah, and Muhammad is the Prophet of God. Come to prayer!' Sindbad repeated these words twice as was ordained. Moreover, the great captain had a fine voice and he loved to hear it.

Below on deck the sailors hurried towards him. The whole ship's company then turned with their faces in that direction where Mecca must lie. Mecca, the Holy City. Now they prayed aloud. As always, they began with *'al Fatiha'*, the first Sura of the Koran, the first verse of which is called the *'basmala'* and goes:

'. . . *bismi llahi al-rahmani al-rahimi* . . .'

Five times a day!

Without their shoes, the whole crew! They said the morning prayer at the first light of dawn in the east; the midday prayer; the afternoon prayer, one hour and a half before sunset; the evening prayer, immediately after sunset; and two hours later, the night prayer.

'Allahu akbar!'

And the slender ship, the graceful dhow of the great Sindbad ran southwards and ever southwards with a favourable wind.

There were no storms. There was no mutiny. No pirate sails were to be seen on the horizon. And so, after many beautiful days, Ali, who was keeping look-out up the mast, crowed:

'Land!—Land!—Land ahead!'

Sailors' feet drummed like thunder on the deck and Sindbad cried with a joyful voice:

'That is Qalah! Come below, little friend. Now you have seen Qalah with your very eyes!'

78

An old sailor climbed the rope-ladder to the crow's-nest. He had to watch out for hidden rocks, countercurrents, the set of the tide and whirlpools. At the same time the men all stood by the ropes, ready to brace the sail. Sindbad had only to give a sign.

About midday the wind began to drop. The ship crept forward slowly. But there did not appear to be any dangerous current around the rocks. They were so close now that they could see the great cloud of birds which rose and sank over the island like a mist.

'I can smell the land,' said Ali, sniffing the air.

Sindbad laughed. 'That is Qalah, little friend. Now you will soon have to dig for the magic lamp.'

A sailor lay over the bow, casting a line in the water. A piece of lead was fastened to the end of it. He drew it out of the water and cried:

'No bottom here, captain!'

'Go on with it!' commanded Sindbad. The sailor rolled the line around his left arm and then threw it again forward.

'I can hear the scream of the birds,' said Ali. He eyed keenly the cliffs which gradually rose up before them.

'Now I also can hear something,' said the captain, 'and I don't like it. Listen carefully.'

Ali held his breath and then panted: 'There is a sound in the air——'

'It's the surf,' nodded Sindbad. 'And it doesn't sound too friendly,' he growled, 'we must approach Qalah from the north.' He held his head on one side, listening. They could hear a dull rumbling, a faint roar.

'It is not coming from there,' said Sindbad. He pointed with outstretched arm to the white rim at the base of the towering cliffs. 'There is no reef there. There is not much surf. Where does the sound of thunder come from?'

Ali stood listening at the rail.

Sindbad shouted a few commands. The slack sail rustled down the mast and flopped on to the main deck. A foresail was rigged along the stout rope running from the bow to the mast.

'Great Sindbad,' said Ali, 'do you hear? The nearer we get to the cliffs the weaker that sound in the air.'

'You are right, little friend,' answered Sindbad. The sound indeed seemed to grow fainter. 'It must be the surf on the other side,' he said.

'Heavy surf?' asked Ali.

'The sea breaking on the rocks,' came the answer.

'If we can hear it from here,' said Ali after a moment's thought, 'then the island can't be very big?'

'Right again, my young friend. We shall certainly make a sailor of you!' said Sindbad. 'They say that Qalah is only a hollow ring of rocks, quite small in circumference.' He turned his head and cried:

'Larboard anchor clear!'

Two sailors ran to it and pulled the iron anchor to the left of the bow. A third bent over the anchor-cable, arranging it so that it would run out smoothly.

The ship behaved like an animal, darting first to one side and then to the other. But not for long; they were soon caught by the land wind. Ali could feel the current of air blowing down on them from the rocky walls. He noticed how the foresail stiffened in the blast and then filled. The *Prince Omar* continued on her way. And one after the other, the man at the mast and the sailor with the line called:

'Level beach ahead!'

'Smooth sand!'

With long strides Sindbad ran to the helm. Single-handed, he steered his dhow towards the narrow belt of foam lining the beach. He gave a signal. The sail was lowered. The sea washed round the ship and ran up along the sand, breaking in little harmless waves and then flowing back.

'Let go the anchor!' roared Sindbad and, with a turn of the tiller, he laid his dhow alongside the beach.

The chain clanked and rattled; the anchor fell, splashing, into a wave. At one moment the *Prince Omar* was running freely; in the next the anchor had gripped the bottom. The sailors hauled, shouting, at the cable. Rocking, the ship came to rest by the beach.

'Qalah!' cried Sindbad. He waved his arms in enthusiasm.

'*Allahu akbar!*' shouted the sailors.

On both sides of the dhow sea-birds thrashed the waves with their wings. In screaming clouds they flew around. The sun disappeared behind them; from their wet feathers fell a rain, wetting ship and crew.

'Allah be praised!' said Sindbad. 'We have reached Qalah. And not a moment too soon!' He looked towards the west. 'The sun is setting. Collect wood from the beach to make a fire, and water,' he cried as he sprang overboard.

Ali followed like a bouncing ball, his black hair flying in the air. The water splashed up round him. He laughed and waded behind the sailor to the beach.

VI

Stones for bread!
King?—No, slave!
Vultures where doves flew;
Wolves instead of sheep . . .

◆ ◆

ETWEEN the sea and the cliffs a fire flickered. Sind-bad's sailors had found some driftwood, the Negro magician a trickle of fresh water in the rocks. And now the ship's company slept here and there on the sand, which was still warm from the heat of the day. They had drunk some coffee and swallowed some gruel; the following day they were to explore Qalah, the enchanted island of which they had heard so much.

Ali did not want to lie down just yet. He sat by the fire opposite the captain. His eyes shone in the light of the glowing embers. Now and then he poked them with a piece of wood and the leaping flames threw Sindbad's gigantic shadow darting about the wall of cliff behind him.

'Early tomorrow morning, little friend,' said the sailor, who was in good spirits, 'you will have to climb these rocks. You, all alone.' He pointed behind him with his thumb.

'Alone?—I—all—alone?' asked the boy, drawing out the words.

Sindbad nodded and resumed: 'It is said that whoever will land on Qalah must send in advance up the cliffs a boy who has neither father nor mother. You have no parents, little friend, light of my eyes.'

'So that is why you raised no objection to taking me with you on this voyage, O wise Sindbad,' grinned Ali, 'not because of Abu Bekr's words.'

'True enough,' laughed the sailor. His beard glowed red in the firelight. 'You will thus be the first human being to look over the top of Qalah's cliffs down into the beautiful garden of Allah, never yet seen by mortal eye. Moreover, little friend, you will then be very close to Aladdin's lamp.'

'I will climb like a monkey, great Sindbad!' answered Ali enthusiastically.

'Now lie down and go to sleep, my son,' commanded the wiry captain. He stood up. 'Sleep and gather strength for the coming day. It will be a great day for us!'

'Where are you going?' Ali wanted to know; he stretched himself lazily on the sand near the dying fire.

The famous captain did not take the question amiss. 'Over to my ship,' he said in an undertone. 'I must study for many hours the position of the stars so that with their help I can make sure of finding this island a second time. Good night, little friend. Sweet dreams of Aladdin's lamp.'

The little brown-skinned beggar pillowed his head in his arms and closed his eyes. He could hear Sindbad splashing in the water. Then the noise stopped; he heard a creaking of taut ropes against the wooden blocks—and then nothing more; only the gentle wash of the waves which licked the shore and then petered out. Then there was the scent of a fire in the open, the taste of the smoke on his tongue, and warm, beautifully dry sand under his body. After weeks of smelling nothing but sea air and fish it was truly wonderful. And tomorrow—why not?—he would close his hands over a copper lamp which would fulfil his every wish.

83

He lay, sighing with fatigue and happiness. Just over there, he thought lazily, floats the great sailor's dhow; he himself will be standing on the poop looking at the stars; and the whole thing—man and ship—a mere shadow on the boundless sea. On the other hand, he thought, the wall of cliffs towers up behind me; I have got to climb them tomorrow; I shall be able to look down on Allah's garden —Allah's garden . . .

He was already asleep.

And he dreamed:

He held the lamp in his hands; Aladdin's magic lamp. He closed his fingers round it and thought—in his dream: First, a ship, as fine as the *Prince Omar*—no finer! Next, ten thousand dirhams of gold; he would drop these in his grandmother's lap, piece by piece! She would then never have to beg again. And silk! Bales of silk for his grandmother. And good food, fruit and sweet milk and also dates from Basra. And further, in the dream, one hundred camels for himself—white, long-legged camels from the Hedjaz, for he wanted to make the journey to Hindustan. He laughed out loud in his dream and rubbed the lamp hard with one hand—and the Spirit appeared and said:

'Wake up, little friend! The day is dawning in the east. You have got to climb up the cliffs.'

'To Hindustan!' said Ali, half-asleep.

Then the great Sindbad bent down and shook the little brown dreamer. Ali looked around dismayed and all Sindbad's sailors laughed, for the boy was grasping a water-gourd tightly in his hands.

'And I thought it was the magic lamp,' said Ali, disappointed. He dropped the gourd and the water gurgled out, making dark patches in the bright-grey sand. The beggar-boy rubbed his eyes.

84

'Here are coffee and dates,' cried the cook.

'Eat and drink, little friend,' said Sindbad, laughing. 'You will soon have to climb up the rocks. Come on.'

Sindbad had said it was going to be a really great day. And it was a great day. But not as the crew had imagined. They now stood at the foot of the cliffs and stared up at the climbing cabin-boy. Around his waist the captain had tied a rope, which was being pulled upwards in jerks.

'He really is as nimble as a monkey!' cried Sindbad.

'There are plenty of clefts and gullies in these rocks,' mumbled the black sailor, 'which the lad can make use of.'

While they were chattering, Ali, high up, disappeared from sight.

'Now he is over the crest,' said a sailor, tugging in astonishment at his bristly beard. They watched the rope that swung about against the deserted face of the cliff.

'He must have tied it to a crag,' said Sindbad with satisfaction. 'We shall soon all be able to climb up into the clouds. Allah's garden will then lie at our feet!'

The men stood motionless, their heads in their necks and their short beards in the air. Up above nothing was to be seen but the jagged crest with the sky above it tinged pink in the gathering light. Some birds swept over, their screams distant and forlorn. Of the cabin-boy Ali there was no sign whatever.

'What can the lad be dawdling about like this for?' growled Sindbad. The sailors continued to stare upwards in silence.

'There he is!' suddenly cried the black-skinned sailor. 'There must be something wrong; he is coming back.'

'Allah is great!' said the captain. 'He is taking hold of the rope.'

The long rope swung violently. They could see the

nimble lad pushing with his feet against the rocks and in fits and starts, like a raindrop on a window-pane, slipping down the cliff-side.

'Allah!' panted Ali just above their heads. He let go the rope and rolled down on to the sand amongst the crew. He then jumped up and, hopping from one foot to the other, blew on his open hands and gasped: 'Phew! phew! That burns like hell-fire!'

'Why did you come back?' asked Sindbad impatiently.

'Because,' panted Ali, '. . . because—Allah!—it burns worse than ten stolen pancakes!' He shook his hands and began to dance about again; they gasped: 'I fastened the rope up there——'

'Talk sense!' ordered the sailor, who had by now lost his patience. 'Speak up! What did you see?'

'See?' sniffed Ali. 'What did I see—up there——'

'Where else, blockhead!' cried Sindbad furiously.

'Nothing . . .' panted Ali. 'I saw nothing, O Sindbad,' he breathed again on his injured palms and said: 'not the slightest sign of any wonderful garden——'

'This is no time for joking,' roared the captain. 'Any more nonsense and I'll beat you black and blue!' He took the lad by the scruff of his neck and shook him.

'Let me go, O Sindbad, let me go,' whimpered Ali, wriggling; then when the sailor's anger had abated a little: 'Great Sindbad! Whatever may be the name of this island, it is not Qalah.'

'Hold your tongue, young puppy!' said Sindbad growing angry again. Frightened, Ali ran a short distance, then turned and called:

'Climb up yourself, great Sindbad. You will see for yourself!'

'Come here at once!' cried the sailor. He made a gesture as if to a slave. 'Come and report all you have seen in its proper order. Come!'

Ali crept forward step by step on the pale sand as he gasped: 'On the other side of the cliff—great Sindbad—are you going to hit me?—on the other side—there are only rocks and boulders—and nothing more . . .' He remained at a safe distance. 'Down below is a bay and there is the surf we heard yesterday. One or two goats were wandering about and—I saw two men. One is as tall as you, great Sindbad, perhaps even taller—his beard is as white as milk. The other man is short and fat like a filled water-skin. But no ship—nothing—and no lovely garden with green grass——'

'Shaitan, that evil Prince of Darkness, has played one of his tricks on us!' cried Sindbad, stamping his foot on the sand.

'. . . . and—O Sindbad!' said Ali, 'there is no need for you to climb the rope to see all this. This beach,' he pointed to the sand, 'continues all round to the bay behind the cliffs, passing through the rocks. There the men are, busy with something or other, the fat one and the one with the white beard.'

'In that case,' said the sailor, 'we will go and have a look at these fellows. Allah help you, little brown beggar, if you are not telling the truth!' He shook his fist and rolled his eyes. Then he called out:

'Listen, men! You, Ibrahim and you, Husain and also you—' he pointed at the black sailor—'you will remain on watch by the ship. Fill the skins with fresh water—all of them. The others follow me. Quick march!'

Cursing, he stumped ahead of his motley band over the low sand-dunes. The men followed. The morning breeze blew out their trousers and fluttered the red and green rags they wore round their heads. On their right screaming flocks of sea-birds rose from the water; above them the air hummed with beating wings. Beside them, the sailors' long shadows twisted in the undulating sand.

After a short time they reached the westerly side of the island where they found some footprints; then, a little later, they rounded a great rock and stopped, stock-still.

'Now you can see for yourself,' said Ali in an undertone. The sailors, on the other hand, stared ahead with open mouths muttering 'Ah!' and gasping 'Oh!'

The bay lay before them.

On one side crumbling cliffs jutted out and were lost in the sea. To their right the surf thundered, rolling between sharp fragments of rock. Behind this girdle of foam and whirlpools lay a calm stretch of water; it looked like a small lake, the grim overhanging cliffs reflected on its dark surface.

Three or four goats were moving about on a boulder-strewn slope, dotted with small clumps of green. Behind them a black buck was just disappearing into a cleft which ran out into the sea.

'Two men!' growled Sindbad.

These were standing at the end of the bay, their arms hanging by their sides. They looked across but made no movement as Sindbad and his sailors marched towards them along the water's edge. And the one was just as fat and the other's beard just as white as Ali had said.

Ali could now see that both the strangers were covered with wretched rags, full of holes and frayed all round the edges. Whitebeard had long and emaciated limbs; his skin was deep brown; his black eyes were wide open and did not waver. The little fat man, on the other hand, hid timidly behind his older companion as the sailors approached.

'Salaam!' said Sindbad, stepping up to Whitebeard. Then he asked: 'Who are you and what are you doing on this island?'

'*Aleikum*,' returned the old man. The wind coming off the cliffs fanned his white beard.

89

'Answer!' commanded Sindbad.

'You are rude, my son!' said the old man. Herewith he drew himself up and at once appeared taller than the wellbuilt Sindbad. Ali, standing at the sailor's side, thought he noticed a smile hovering around the stranger's mouth.

He was surprised at these few words which sounded like music in his ears.

'Your name?' asked Sindbad. Ali was astonished that the captain showed no anger.

'My name is Asoka, and I am the ambassador of the Shah-in-shah of Hindustan. Who are you, my friend?'

Hindustan! thought Ali, hopping from one foot to the other. He said Hindustan! And again he felt the bittersweet feeling under his skin which came whenever he heard this word.

'I am Sindbad,' said the sailor. 'My fame has spread throughout all the seas of the world!' He pointed over his shoulder. 'That is my crew.' The sailors, however, for their part were astounded to hear their captain give such detailed answers to an old and ragged stranger.

'This is my servant,' said Whitebeard. He turned round to his fat companion. 'Don't be afraid, Rahulo,' he said, smiling. 'These men are kind and friendly.'

'Pirates!' squeaked the little man in a voice that could scarcely escape from his throat.

'Pirates! We?' asked Sindbad threateningly. He took a step forward.

But the old man laid a hand on the captain's left shoulder and said: 'Take no notice of his words, my son.' Under his breath, so that the timid one could not understand, he added: 'Rahulo, my servant, is sick. His thoughts are often disordered. He has lived with me on this island for ten years; he has been tortured several times; for we are prisoners here.'

'Prisoners?' cried Sindbad; now Ali could read anger and hatred in his eyes. 'Who has dared? Who are those that dare to keep you prisoner, honourable sir?' He gripped the hilt of his scimitar which hung in its curved sheath against his blue trousers. 'Show them to me and I will crush them!'

'Be calm, my son,' answered the old man, smiling. 'Leave your weapon where it is.' With outstretched arm he pointed across the belt of surf towards the open sea. 'Our enemies are out there with three ships on a voyage of piracy.'

The sailors all turned their heads, but the horizon lay empty and uniform under the bright morning sky; no sail was anywhere to be seen. Sindbad assumed an expression as hard as flint and asked in a hoarse voice:

'So this island, which I thought was Qalah, is nothing but a nest of evil vultures?'

'That is so, my friend,' nodded the old man, but this time he did not smile. 'This island is certainly not named Qalah; they call it Mullak.'

'And what, worthy sir,' asked Sindbad hastily, 'is the device they carry on their flag?'

'It is a circular disc,' said Whitebeard, 'red on a yellow background. I have often seen this flag flying from their dhows . . .'

'That is the band of the blood-red moon!' groaned the great Sindbad, at which he went as pale as the sand beneath his feet. 'Allah! We have no minute to lose! This island is accursed.'

'It is so,' said the old man, 'you are certainly right, my friend. Turn back and weigh anchor before the pirates return. My servant and I—I pray you, my son—take us with you in your ship.'

'Of course!' cried the sailor. 'And you shall pay nothing for the voyage!'

'You will be rewarded for your service, friend,' replied the old man. He then laid his gaunt hand on the crooked shoulder of his fat servant and said to him: 'Rahulo, go with these men; I will follow shortly. We are going to escape from misery and want. These men are our friends.'

'Pirates?' piped the fat fellow, rolling his eyes in fear.

'Friends!' affirmed the old man, and he gave a good-natured smile. Then the timid one seized the nearest sailor with his little hands and clung to him, giggling, nodding and whining. Whitebeard, however, strode towards the cliffs and disappeared into a cave as high as himself.

'Allah!' cried Sindbad. 'What caves! This is just the place for stolen gold and precious stones. Attention, all of you!' He divided his people into parties to search for the pirates' loot. A look-out was posted up on the rocks. To his cabin-boy the great captain said:

'You have the fleetest legs of us all. Run and tell Ibrahim to make the *Prince Omar* ship-shape and ready to sail at a moment's notice.'

'I once ran with a hot pancake,' said Ali, making off across the bay and over the boulders, his black hair streaming like a pennant.

In no time he had reached the rocks at the westerly point of the island and scrambled through them like a hare with the hounds after him. And as he ran on, scraps of words raced through his head, words dropped by the white-bearded one.

In front of him lay the undulating sandy beach, so

spongy that he sank up to his ankles and found it difficult to make progress. Once he fell and a wave broke over his head and tried to drag him seawards. He spluttered, gasped and scrambled ashore. He ran on, waving his arms and grunting with his effort.

Supposing, he thought, that the pirates come before our people are on board? If the ship is even in sight of the island when they come? He suddenly stumbled and fell with his arms outstretched. He spat the sand out of his mouth and carefully turned his head.

'Allah!' he said, 'that's Husain——'

Then his whole body began to shake, his limbs trembled; for between the shoulder-blades of the sailor lying close by on the sand, was stuck the hilt of a dagger.

Ali raised himself slowly on to his knees. Goose-flesh crept over his back, from his waist right up to the top of his head. There, quite near him, to the right, a water-skin had emptied itself, except for a few drops around the opening. A few paces away some drops of water glistened in the grey rock. And there, on the left, there lay Husain, the sailor, like a log—dead; only a fragment of green cloth behind his ear waved in the wind.

His next thought was of Ibrahim, the other sailor; he must call him. He squeezed between the dead man and the cliffs and ran as fast as if the devil were at his heels. But only for a couple of hundred paces! Then the little beggar came to a sudden stop, panting for breath. He could not believe his eyes!

The *Prince Omar* was no longer anchored near the shore. Without a sail the ship was drifting slowly away out to sea; she floated a good stone's throw from the water's edge. Sea-birds were circling round the empty mast, shining like silver in the morning light. Aft, on the poop, stood two men, looking far from friendly. Ali recognized Ibrahim and the black wizard. They went for one another. Now they had fallen; the lad heard the thud on the wooden deck.

Ali then dived head-first into the water. As he swam he had to fight the swell which, although not strong, was enough to swamp him. With all his strength he swam after the dhow. The ship loomed dark against the brilliant sky and rocked gently. It was drifting; a current was carrying it gradually away from the island of Mullak.

Later, Ali used to say that he swam as fast as a fish. That no doubt was an exaggeration. However, at last his head bumped against the *Prince Omar's* hard hull. He found himself beneath the stern of the ship, so with a few breast-strokes made for the starboard side. Meanwhile he could hear the dreadful oaths of the fighting sailors interspersed with heavy blows. He gripped the rudder, which in dhows is fixed to the side, and pulled himself up. He slid back; the wood was as slippery as soap. Again he tried, and a third time. At last he managed to reach the spar running through the rudder and was able to clamber over the side on to the main deck.

And not a moment too soon!

He could see the Negro kneeling on Ibrahim's chest, and saw their entwined hands. It was obvious that Ibrahim was getting the worst of it. Ali dragged a belaying-pin from the locker by the mast and rushed up the ladder on to the poop. With a cry of anger he raised the belaying-pin above his head and brought it down with a crash on the humped back of the wizard.

There they stood; Ali, the cabin-boy and Ibrahim, the sailor; and between them, lying on the deck with closed eyes, the black man.

94

'Have I killed him?' asked Ali in gasps; he thought, for the moment, he was going to be sea-sick again.

'No—but he will be unconscious for a while,' said Ibrahim, wiping blood and sweat from his face with the back of his hand.

'He has stabbed Husain,' said Ali. 'Over there by the spring. I could see the hilt of a dagger.'

'The son of a dog!' panted the sailor. 'Sindbad will hang him at the mast-head for this. You came in the nick of time—I was finished. But look, we are drifting out to sea. Help me hoist a sail.'

Together they hoisted a small sail forward. Ali made fast the braces; the sailor took the tiller and steered for the shore.

'How did it all happen?' Ali wanted to know.

'That's soon told,' was Ibrahim's answer. 'I saw that Shaitan go with Husain to the spring and, shortly after, he came back with his water-skin, but Husain was not with him. He carried the filled skin on board, called me and, pointing to the anchor-cable, said: "What do you think would happen if I cut it?" I said: "There is a slight current here which would carry the ship away from the island." Then he said: "I'll try it," took up an axe and cut the rope. The *Prince Omar* began at once to drift. The dog said to me: "Do you see that sail on the horizon, Ibrahim?"— pointing eastwards. And as I turned my head away he tried to get me with the axe but missed; I went for him and we were still at it when you came along, little friend.'

'A sail?' cried Ali, seizing the sailor by the arm.

At this moment the bow of the ship touched the shore; Ibrahim put the tiller over. 'Take hold of the anchor-rope and jump overboard,' he ordered.

They were soon both splashing through the water, hauling on the same rope. This they made fast to a huge boulder as high as a man. Then Ibrahim said:

'Now our ship is safe again. Come, let's tie up the dog there; otherwise as soon as he comes to he will make off. Then we must give poor Husain a decent burial.'

'The sail!' said Ali. 'What was that about a sail, Ibrahim? Did you really see a sail?' He fidgeted with impatience.

'Use your eyes, Ali!' laughed the sailor. He slowly raised his arm and pointed to the eastern horizon. 'There!' he said. 'Or are they perhaps clouds?'

In the east little triangles could be seen between water and sky, but difficult to recognize in the shimmering light.

Ali counted in a hoarse voice: 'One—two—three. There are three sails.'

'You say that as if they were ghosts,' grinned the sailor.

'Allah!' breathed the little beggar, growing pale with fear. 'They are pirates, Ibrahim. The band of the red moon.'

'The band of the red moon?' echoed the sailor; he took Ali by the shoulders and, shaking him roughly, cried: 'How do you know that, boy?'

'This island—it isn't Qalah,' stammered the lad. 'It is called Mullak and is a pirates' haunt.'

'Then we must get out of here like the wind!' gasped Ibrahim. And Ali said: 'I'm off!'

He ran off across the sandy beach and the low dunes. When he came up to where the silent Husain lay in the sand and saw the screaming birds flapping round him, he stooped down and threw a couple of stones at them. Then, as he ran, he thought: the captain sent a man up the cliffs; I hope this man has also noticed the strange sails.

It had been as Ali hoped. Half-way between the ship and the bay he could see people. They were running and Sindbad the Sailor was far ahead of them.

'Faster!' crowed the little beggar. 'Run faster, great Sindbad! There are three sails in the east.'

'I know,' panted the sailor.

Ali, running alongside him, gasped: 'The sailors move like snails. Order them to hurry or we may be too late!'

'Their pockets are full of gold pieces, all of them,' coughed the sailor and added: 'Gold and silver from a cave—that's why they can't move quickly.' And now Ali understood why the trousers of the great Sindbad himself were bulging so. In spite of the screaming birds the lad could hear the coins in his clothes clinking at every step he took. He said:

'You have found the pirates' treasure, great Sindbad?'

'And what a treasure!' panted the captain. 'But spare your breath,' he ordered; then he stumbled and went on: 'so many boxes and chests filled with gold and silver—it is astonishing!'

Man and boy approached the little cape where the spring trickled out of a cleft in the rock. Ali gave a quick look but could not see the dead Husain any longer. 'Allah be praised!' he said.

'What in the name of the devilish Shaitan'—cursed Sindbad—'what are those lazy dogs doing? There's no sail at the mast!' He plodded forward angrily. Round the cape the bare mast of the dhow pointed to the sky. 'Didn't you give Ibrahim my orders?' asked the captain, threateningly. 'To get ready to sail, all sails should be——'

'Great Sindbad,' said Ali quickly, 'it isn't possible. Ibrahim is alone on board—that is—the wizard is also on board—tied up—because he stabbed Husain—he tried to kill Ibrahim and they had a terrible fight—then I got there —you will hear all about it—Allah!' the lad panted and stood stock-still. 'There they are—all three of them . . .'

'Nearer than I thought,' murmured Sindbad. He also stopped and stared eastwards, where three dhows could be clearly seen in the morning light. By now the sailors had come up; they cursed and swore as they caught sight of the sails.

'They are changing course,' said the captain. 'We are already discovered; they are standing by for us.' Turning his head, he shouted: 'Hurry! Run like mad! They are coming!' He led the way with his long legs, the gold clinking against his limbs.

The *Prince Omar* was tugging at the cable like a shying horse. Every time a wave rolled under her, she reared. Her

bow rose and crashed down again into the water; foam
ran along the gunwale; sometimes the spray shot up into
the air and showered down on to the deck.

The first to clamber aboard the pounding ship was
Sindbad. He roared an order at the waiting Ibrahim. Next,
he gave a kick at the wizard, lying bound on the deck.
Then the famous sailor ran to the tiller.

The sailors, with their laden pockets and heavy bundles,
clambered over the gunwale. Some still splashed about
between the ship and the shore. They made enough noise
to waken the dead.

Ali alone remained on dry ground by the camping site.
He waited for the whitebearded man, who had been left
far behind. With firm strides he approached, tall and
ragged, his white beard flying in the breeze.

In front of the dead fire he stopped. Putting a lean hand to his eyes, he gazed out to sea; his look never wavered although the distant sails sparkled like crystal in the brilliant sunlight.

'Your servant is already on board, honoured father,' said Ali, looking up at the ancient face.

'I saw him wading to the ship with the sailors, my friend,' answered the old man. He stood still, breathing deeply.

'We must go, sir,' pressed Ali. 'Let me carry your bundle,' he added pointing to the knotted cloth the old man held in his left hand.

'Take it,' said Whitebeard.

Side by side they ploughed through the waves which came up to their waists.

'The swell is increasing,' panted Ali. 'I was swimming less than an hour ago and the waves were not half so high then.'

Willing hands pulled them aboard. The old man was dragged over the dripping timbers. No sooner were his legs over the gunwale than Ali followed, as nimble as a cat.

The mainboom and the sail were hauled into position. Tilting against the sky, the great triangular sail flapped about until the sailors ran to the braces; then it caught the wind and filled out. Under pressure of the strong breeze, the *Prince Omar* now lay over towards the land. Deep down in the hull the wooden spars and braces creaked and groaned; the whole ship shuddered and behaved like an animal trembling with fear.

Sindbad dashed across the deck, drawing his curved scimitar from its sheath. With one blow he severed the straining cable. The vessel immediately left the shore and plunged into the rolling waves, sending a shower of spray over the sailors.

'Allah!' cried the whole crew with gaping mouths.

The captain gave an order. The helmsman heaved against the tiller and swung the dhow into the wind. Only now could Sindbad mount the poop to survey the pirates. Here also Whitebeard was standing, holding on to the stern-rail. Sindbad gazed eastwards and said to the old man:

'We have lost too much time. Their sails are distinctly nearer. The question now is their rig. I can't recognize it from this distance.'

'Single-masted,' said Whitebeard. 'They have the same rig as this ship, my son.'

'Allah be praised!' Sindbad sighed with relief. And, turning to Ali who was helping the crew, he said: 'Hi, lazy bones! Run to my cabin and fetch a cloth to dry the worthy one; he is soaked through and is cold.'

Ali did as he was bid. In the meantime the old man had untied the bundle which the lad had carried through the water for him. Sindbad opened his eyes wide; for in the old man's hand rolled a good dozen or so large and flawless pearls, shining like silk in the sunlight.

'The finest pearls I have ever seen!' gasped the captain.

Whitebeard nodded and said: 'These pearls are not mine. They belong to the Shah-in-shah of Hindustan, whose ambassador I am. When, ten years ago, he sent me on this journey he gave me the pearls to pay for my food, drink and lodging on the way. Our ship was attacked by pirates on the high seas and plundered. Only I and my poor servant Rahulo remained alive and we were brought to the barren island of Mullak. The pirate chief, however, stole the pearls; but I knew where he had hidden them. Now I have them again; none are missing.'

'Allah works miracles!' said Sindbad.

'Three,' added the old man, 'and for my servant Rahulo three others. Take them; they are yours, my son!' He tried to press six of the pearls into Sindbad's brown hand. But the sailor put both his hands behind his back and said: 'You do not need to pay anything, honoured sir, and nor does your childish servant. Once upon a time these pearls would have been worth more to me than the fares of a hundred men in my ship. Now I am rich and my sailors not less so; we found whole heaps of gold and silver in the pirates' cave.' He turned his head and looked out across the sea; then he said: 'Moreover, it is by no means certain that this ship will be able to escape those three sails. Allah alone knows whether my ship will ever again drop anchor in Bagdad.'

Just then the fat Rahulo toddled towards them and, pointing with his plump little hand to the east, piped: 'Pirates!'

Sindbad looked up at the masthead and said to Ali: 'Up aloft, little friend. A rope is jammed up there. Loosen it! Ibrahim must hoist our flag.'

Hand over hand Ali climbed to the crow's-nest. The flag came up from below through his legs, swept across his bare body and opened out at the top of the mast, green and fluttering.

From his airy height the cabin-boy had a good look round, the wind tousling his black hair. In the distance he could see white dots dancing, foam-crested waves. It was scarcely midday and the hot sun poured down on the rushing watery waste. But in the east, was not the horizon colouring up like a sword at the smithy's? That might easily mean a storm.

And now, what was this? Ali could clearly see flags

hoisted, one after the other, on the pirate ships. Red spots that suddenly appeared above the bright sails. Dancing red patches, one moment there and the next moment gone, as if they were signalling to the green flag. The wind carried away the outcry raised by the sailors below. Then Ali slid down the mast and, when he had reached the stern, he heard Whitebeard say: 'What do you think of it, my son?'

The great Sindbad scratched his beard, frowned and replied:

'Ahead there is no land until the African coast. But that is too far for us; there is not much water on board and not enough dates or flour. I have therefore decided to hold on this westerly course until night time. Then, under cover of the darkness, we will change course towards the north. Perhaps in this way we may escape.'

'I have often listened to these pirates talking,' said Whitebeard, 'about sailing and seamanship. From that I know that there are some low islands ahead of us; coral reefs, running from north to south. There must be a terrible surf there.'

'How far ahead?' asked Sindbad quickly.

'Half a day's journey from Mullak to westward.'

'Allah protect us!' cried the sailor. 'In that case these dogs are driving us into a trap.'

The old man nodded. 'Many a ship do they force on to those malevolent reefs. Once a ship is stranded, they board and plunder it. If one should avoid the reefs they fall on it all together and attack it.'

'We are as good as lost!' murmured Sindbad, and added: 'Is there any advice, O most worthy one, that you can offer in this desperate situation?'

Whitebeard smiled. With his hand to his forehead, he gazed back eastwards.

A stretch of sea, perhaps wide enough for a fast dhow to traverse in an hour, separated Sindbad's ship from the pirates. Since they had sailed, the swell had greatly increased. White crests were everywhere to be seen. Gradually, almost unnoticeably, the sun began to lose its power; the burning disc of the midday sky was becoming veiled in mist and clouds.

'There is only one thing to do, my son,' said the old man. 'Don't hold on a true westerly course. Let your ship bear to the north. There is going to be a storm.'

'A storm and coral reefs ahead!' said Sindbad hoarsely. 'That will be the end of us! If on the other hand I bear north, then I am shortening the distance for those hellhounds on the horizon! They will catch us then like sharks the small-fry.'

'If you change course now, it will certainly be to their advantage,' said Whitebeard calmly. 'Yes, then they will attack the ship. They carry Greek Fire, my son, and they also have bows and arrows. In this sea a good shot will reach the target. That is why I say, don't change course suddenly, but gradually bear northwards. They can then only approach slowly.'

'But in the end they will come alongside just the same—and my sailors are no soldiers!' muttered Sindbad dejectedly.

'Yes, my son,' answered the old man, stroking his beard. 'But that is the only way you can avoid the reefs and beat the storm.'

'What do you mean by that, worthy one?' asked Sindbad in surprise.

'The waves will get higher and higher,' was the answer. 'In an hour's time they will perhaps begin to break. We shall be in the midst of a storm. Then change direction and bear northwards. It is true that our enemies will get closer; but they will need many hands to deal with the storm. There will be fewer to fight us. In addition to that, it is only by mere chance that you can hit a man with an arrow or a ship with fire in a storm, when the sea is really rough.'

'Allah!' cried the captain. 'We shall do as you say, O worthy one!' He twirled his moustache and said to his cabin-boy:

'Come, little friend! Come and help me distribute the bows, as many arrows as you have fingers and a cutlass for each man.'

By the rail, near the ladder, lay the magician. He made an angry grimace as Sindbad passed him. The captain stopped and, giving him a kick, said to Ali:

'As soon as you have distributed the weapons you must come and tell me in detail all the mischief this devil has caused.'

This Ali did.

Then the magician was dragged amidships. Sindbad, surrounded by his sailors, tried to question him. The man only made ugly grimaces and Sindbad had to get the whole story out of Ali and Ibrahim.

'This son of the devil,' cried Sindbad, 'is a traitor. When he saw the pirates coming, he stabbed my man, Husain. Then he cut my ship adrift and tried to kill my man, Ibrahim. In this way the pirates would have been able to board my ship without resistance. We should all by now have been either dead or prisoners on the island of Mullak. Has anyone anything to say?'

He looked around the circle. The men murmured threateningly. Ibrahim spoke:

'Great Sindbad! It must be said that all this would have happened but for our cabin-boy. My strength was giving out. Ali came to the rescue and knocked this man down. I was then able to steer the ship ashore; otherwise I should be as dead now as my friend Husain.'

'Allah!' cried the sailors.

The captain said: 'It is so, Ibrahim. And you,' he turned and laid a hand on the beggar-boy's head, 'you have brought us good luck, little friend, light of my eyes. I thank you!'

Ali thought to himself: Now he calls me 'little friend'. A few hours ago he threatened to beat me black and blue and called me 'little dog'. He grinned, his teeth flashing. The sailors thought he was smiling with pride because the famous captain had given him such praise.

'What shall be done with this dog?' Sindbad asked.

'Hang him!' cried several sailors.

'Overboard with him!' said Ibrahim.

'Very well!' agreed the captain. 'There is no time for ceremony. Away with him!'

Giving vent to their wrath, the sailors dragged the bound man to starboard.

Ali turned and ran up the steps. As he ran he heard the body splash into the water. He shuddered with horror and grasped the stern-rail with both hands. He saw a bundle of clothes twisting about; then came a huge wave rolling over it, which a second later thundered with a foaming crest against the stern of the ship.

Ali closed his eyes as the water poured over, drenching him. When he turned round he found himself looking straight into the strong calm face of the old man.

'That was . . .' stammered the youth.

'What was it, young friend?' asked the old man. His voice was deep, like the tolling of a bell.

'Terrible!' Ali decided. He shuddered again.

'Yes,' nodded Whitebeard. 'They repaid evil with evil. The sailor, whom you saw drown, was a member of the pirate band which is pursuing us. I saw him often enough on the island of Mullak and recognized him again today. He was many times in ships sailing these waters, and used to deliver sailors who were strange to them over to the knives of his cruel friends.'

'And you said nothing about this, worthy one?'

'Would it have saved the unfortunate man?' the old man wanted to know.

'No,' Ali admitted, hanging his head. His long black hair fell over his eyes. 'No, worthy one. He would still have had to die and they would have handled him still more roughly.'

The old man bowed his head in acknowledgement.

Sindbad then came up to survey the pirates.

'Their ships are still a good way off,' said the old man.

'Yes,' agreed Sindbad. 'But look aft. They have already

noticed that we are bearing north. There—the sail nearest us—he is trying to cut us off.'

After a time it became more difficult to keep an eye on the pirates. The following waves were constantly increasing in size. Every time the water struck the stern, the whole ship shook and groaned in all its joints. It plunged and reared and staggered in the troughs between the waves.

Far more quickly than had been expected, the storm was upon them. The highest waves began to break; clouds of foam drove westwards across the sea. Whistling, the wind tore ribbons of water from their crests. Added to this, a faint twilight descended on them. Looking towards the sun made one sea-sick; only the mast and slanting boom, black strips swinging against a sulphurous background, were to be seen.

'It is now too late to turn northwards,' cried Sindbad, his words hardly audible against the almost continuous howling of the gale. 'Come,' he called, and, taking the old man by the arm, led him along the groaning deck and down below the companion-way, out of the wind. Ali followed. The three of them drew breath.

The sailors were already crouching wherever they could find protection from the storm.

'You will have to change course, my son,' breathed the old man. 'Otherwise you will strike the coral reefs. Who knows how close they are already?'

'Allah alone knows,' replied Sindbad. 'Only Allah can now save my ship. There is nothing we can do.'

He leaned against the wall of the cabin and crossed his arms.

'Give the order to change course,' said Whitebeard; his look was clear and penetrating.

'What! Athwart this storm?' cried Sindbad. 'Sail across

this swell—ha! That would be suicide. The first breaker to strike the hull would shatter the ship; the second swamp us! No! We can only hope that Allah will bring our ship safely through the islands. Can't you see that they have reefed the sail down to the merest patch? Even that wouldn't stand against this gale!'

Ali was frightened when he saw how despondently the famous sailor leaned against the woodwork.

'There is no opening between the reefs,' said Whitebeard. 'Anyone who has tried to find one has struck and sunk.'

'Then Allah protect us!' said Sindbad; and his head banged against the wooden wall.

'No,' said the old man, 'help yourself, my son!'

'It's all over with us,' answered Sindbad, his arms now hanging limp by his side.

'Throw the tiller round!' said Whitebeard. 'There is still time. Turn the ship round and run east-north-east. Come, give the order!'

Ali's eyes opened wide with astonishment; the famous sailor obeying an old man! Sindbad stumbled forward and, cupping his hands round his mouth, cried:

'All hands, prepare to luff!'

Terrified, the sailors got up. They clung to the rigging, to the woodwork, as they gained their stations. Only to starboard, at the tiller, Ibrahim waved and cried:

'You will sink the ship, great Sindbad!'

The captain turned his head, looking round at the old man. Ali thought: He is eyeing Sindbad just as Abu Bekr eyed me. And he heard the deep, clear voice say:

'Take the tiller yourself, Sindbad, my son. Four arms are better than two in weather like this!'

'No skipper has ever dared such a thing,' cried Sindbad

in reply. 'If we luff now we are lost!' He stood perplexed, swaying on his straddled legs.

Then the old man roared so loudly that his words sounded clearly above the storm:

'GO—Sindbad! I order it! I was sailing in storms before you ever saw the light in Saoud!'

The sailors saw how the world-famous ship's master obeyed the whitebeard. So they also obeyed and slouched to their work.

In the teeth of the wind the old man, with flying beard, climbed to the poop. Ali helped him, for the gale tore at his lean body, causing him to tremble.

The old man waited for a number of waves to break against the stern. Then, in a ringing voice, he shouted:

'Let go the braces!' Then, leaning forward over the rail, 'Ship the boom!' A second afterwards: 'Over with the rudder, Sindbad, my son!'

Ali saw the crew cringe and wriggle as if they had been whipped. Below him the two at the tiller bent their backs as they leaned hard against it: Sindbad and Ibrahim. Two great rolling seas approached from the east but they did not break over the hull; instead, they raised the ship to the skies on their crests before dropping her into the troughs. Water streamed over the deck and the sailors stood up to their waists in swirling foam. But everything held fast; there was no great damage.

The *Prince Omar* swung her tilted bow from west to north and then over to north-east and ran, with reefed sail, right into the wind. As the first breaker charged up, a taut foresail had already been hoisted forward. White-beard shouted his order so expertly to the sailors below that the dhow avoided the plunging mass of water.

This was the last command the old man gave. He called

to Sindbad and, himself, climbed down under protection from the gale.

Now the famous sea-captain again took charge of his ship. A young sailor sweated in his place by Ibrahim's side. Ali was told to fetch leather buckets from the hold and distribute them. Everyone whose hands were free baled out the water, for now waves were constantly breaking from windward over the gunwale. Rigging and sails were drenched in foam.

There was no longer sunlight nor colour around the panting men. There was nothing but this swirling waste of grey-green water. The tumultuous seas were veined with bright strips of foam. Sheets of water smacked against the ropes. The whole ship groaned continuously as if Shaitan were playing a dead march. Lowering clouds dipped from the heavens as if they were trying to suffocate the sailors.

The *Prince Omar*, however, ran eastwards—eastwards in spite of everything! The slender bow pounded valiantly against the scourging storm, away from the cruel reefs which, with jagged points, had been waiting for them. And the whitebearded old man on board had been right.

It was during this witches' dance of the plunging ship in a howling gale that the cabin-boy brought off his master-piece. It happened thus.

Whitebeard beckoned to Ali and asked: 'Are you afraid, young friend?'

Ali shook his head. 'No, worthy one,' he said. 'At first, yes. I was almost sick with fear, and when you turned the ship round I thought it was all over.' He grinned and added: 'But nothing is over! We are alive and running into the wind.'

'Hard into the wind,' nodded the old man. Although he

crouched under the companion-way salt water dripped from his beard. Then he stretched out his arm and pointed aloft.

'Are you frightened to climb up there?' he asked.

Ali, squatting beside Whitebeard, followed the arm with his eyes. He noticed that the green flag was frayed and torn in many places. A wave broke over the ladder. Water buffeted him in the face. When he could again open his eyes, the thin arm was still pointing up at the whining rigging. Then Ali said:

'No, I am not afraid!' He said this, although he was really terribly frightened; he said it, however, because of the compelling power coming from those eyes which looked steadily at him without blinking. He said: 'I will go, worthy one, and see what the pirates are doing.'

'No sailor would dare to do it,' said the old man with a smile. 'You are young and nimble. We must know how near is the enemy, as we are running straight at him. On no account must we come between the ships of the pirates. Now, pay attention . . .' and he showed Ali how to signal with his arms.

'What is going to happen, worthy father?' Ali wanted to know.

The old man answered: 'In this sea they cannot board us. They will, however, shoot arrows at us—pitch and tow—burning arrows. They will be out to annihilate us, as we know their nest—the island of Mullak.'

'Burning arrows, did you say?' asked Ali, grinning. All at once he felt the strength return to his knees. 'I'll go!' he cried, getting up and steadying himself against the ladder.

'Go and take a new rope with you,' shouted Sindbad from the poop.

Ali nodded and bounded away.

'Fasten yourself securely!' called Sindbad after him. The lad was already busy by a hatch.

He knew the hold inside out, but before he again crept out of the opening he had given himself a dozen bumps and bruises down in the dark under the creaking deck.

'What are you doing with those buckets?' roared Sindbad. His words were lost in the howling wind. The boy was already in the rigging, climbing hand over hand up to the crow's-nest. Two leathern buckets dangled from his back.

The storm tore at his body so that Ali could feel it in every bone. He let the wind press him against the ropes and could then hear the humming that rose from the ship through the rigging. After each shock he had a short rest. Then Ali clenched his teeth and pulled himself a little higher.

He had twisted the rope several times round his body; he now made it fast to the mast, crouching on the slippery bar. In that way he could not fall nor be torn away. Even if the ship swung its mast like a whip, the lad had a firm seat in the crow's-nest.

Sitting thus, he had the roar of the wind in his ears, and the deep organ-notes of the sea. Before his eyes stretched the terrible dark-grey watery waste to the south—behind him to the north—forward to the east. From the east came the storm. From the east came the waves and—three sails! They rode before the wind; sometimes behind bright strips of foam, climbing high immediately afterwards, Three sails! Above each one flew the round full moon, the flag of the pirates.

Ali shouted. He waved. With both arms he waved, and called down to the deck below. There the sailors waded in water; they slipped, fell and crept about like beetles on a piece of meat. The ship, in the meantime, dropped into a

furrow of boiling froth and the enemy was terribly close!

At last! Sindbad had seen the violent signals. The old man waved both hands. Shortly after, the boy noticed that the *Prince Omar* veered a little to the north.

There was no time to lose. One of the pirate ships danced so near now that Ali could have counted the heads on board. He did not count them, however.

Burning arrows the old man had said. Ali grinned and took hold of the leathern buckets he had dragged up over the rigging.

Tow and pitch the old man had said. Very well, then, tow and pitch were in the two buckets. In the hold Ali had already tied them together in such a manner that he could hold the one and let the other swing loose.

Crouching against the cordage, the lad managed to create shelter from the wind by bending double. He fished out tinder and flint from his red loin-cloth. Then began a trying business. Grunting with zeal, Ali struck sparks, tow and touchwood held between his knees. The sparks just would not catch; again he tried, and again; for the tenth time! Ah! At last the tinder glowed. He let it draw in the wind a little until it was well alight.

'Now then,' said Ali, 'now come along with your burning arrows!'

He raised his head and looked straight in front of him. Just to the right a pirate ship came at them out of a wave. One deep valley and one high mountain still separated the two masts. Then everything happened as swiftly as in a dream.

Ali dropped the tinder into the right-hand bucket. Then, held only by the rope, he stood on the bar and swung it with his right arm. He held the other bucket firmly with his left hand.

Then came the first burning arrow, a streak of fire past his streaming black hair. Another came hissing by. Another, three—four—a dozen, all aimed lower.

With a shout, Ali let the right-hand bucket go and then threw the other after it. The pirates' bowsprit at that moment projected over Sindbad's dhow. The ships ran alongside each other, in opposite directions, and Ali could have jumped over to the pirates' vessel. A gust of wind sufficed to part the two ships.

Again Ali shouted aloud. His buckets had fallen right on to the enemy's boom.

One of them caught and hung just under the swelling sail of the pirate. A flame licked up out of the opening, smoke poured forth, and in a moment the sail was alight the whole length of the yard-arm. Pitch ran, burning, along the rigging. Suddenly a gust tore the flaming canvas down the middle. Smoke streamed westward.

'Allah!' panted Ali, letting himself slip back on to the cross-bar. He began to feel quite sick. He thought: They would have made fun of me, the lot of them, if it hadn't come off. And Sindbad would have beaten me on account of the buckets.

He abandoned himself to the gale and looked out over the sea with half-closed eyes.

Two of the pirate ships lay fairly far to the west. They had not been able to reach Sindbad's ship. The third lay close by, stopped and wallowing in the sea, for it was on fire. Ali saw little tongues of flame darting about the rigging; a burning foresail was torn from the mast and fell behind the stern-house.

He thought: The ropes are all tarred against the salt water; the better it will all burn! He closed his eyes and his chin fell on to his bare chest. In his head, a hundred mad thoughts chased one another, rapidly and unhappily.

It was another such world—a sea like this—similar ships —and a gale—daggers stuck in sailors' backs—babbling fat men from Hindustan—burning arrows and islands which were not called Qalah—no—Mullak—and no magic lamp anywhere!

Half an hour later the storm had blown itself out; the wind no longer howled in fiendish gusts. Then the famous sailor Sindbad, single-handed, fetched the half-dead lad down from the crow's-nest. He carried him across the slippery deck and laid him in his own bed in the tiny cabin, and said:

'Allahu akbar!'

VII

A whitebeard from Hindustan—
How steadfast his gaze!
And what a story he has to tell!

◆ ◆

SINDBAD the Sailor kept his dhow on an easterly course until evening and well into the night. The pirate sails had disappeared in the early twilight. The ship sailed without a lantern under a starless sky through the swirling darkness. The storm gradually subsided; by midnight the wind had moderated. But the swell, wave on wave, remained, giving the tired men ample work to do. Moreover, down in the hold, groans could be heard; sailors had been wounded with the burning arrows; two corpses lay covered at the bow.

Up on the poop the great captain paced up and down. He seldom spoke. Every now and then he stood at the stern, grasping the rail. He listened attentively to the night, but could hear only the swirl and sighing of the water as the ship rose and fell. His eyes caught no light nor the shadow of an enemy sail. All the same, Sindbad had asked each man individually whether he carried his cutlass and had bow and arrows within reach.

Meanwhile the cabin-boy slept, breathing hard through his open mouth. Next to him sat the old man who at last, after ten years on the desolate Mullak, was now able to continue his journey.

Ali awoke an hour before daylight, turned his head and half rising, asked:

'Why is it so dark?'

'You are in Sindbad's cabin,' answered the old man's voice. 'We dare not show a light.' Then, after a moment: 'Sleep, young friend, it will soon be morning.'

'I was dreaming,' murmured Ali. He lay back on the pillow, listened to the noise of the water, and finally asked: 'Did I set one of the pirate ships on fire?'

Out of the darkness came the calm reply: 'Yes, you slung two leathern buckets full of burning pitch on to the pirates' mainyard. Sindbad is very proud of you and the sailors call you a hero.'

'Aaah . . .' yawned Ali, 'the air is bad here; these clothes are damp.'

'Sleep,' said the clear voice. 'Sindbad only wants those sailors who are on watch on deck.'

The cabin-boy mumbled something, whereupon the old man said:

'Try to sleep. Breathe through your nose. One should never sleep with an open mouth.' Ali followed with his ears the surging of the swell. He could feel the rhythmical rolling of the ship. And suddenly he said: 'Hindustan——'

'Yes?' came the answer, clear as a bell.

'You are from Hindustan, worthy one!' replied the boy. 'I first heard this name in Bagdad. Mustafa, a story-teller, said something about Hindustan—and—oh, I don't know —I would give my life to be able to go to Hindustan.' Hesitantly he added: 'Will you take me with you as your servant, worthy one?' Ali held his breath, waiting for the answer.

'I shall not be returning home for some time,' replied the old man, 'but if you wish to remain with me then I will give you some clothes and, in addition, a dinar every month.'

'Allah! Will I?' cried the lad. 'And a whole dinar? I had to give that much to the story-teller for some information and he cheated me on top of it!'

'I have learnt from Ibrahim,' said the old man, 'that you are searching for a magic lamp?'

'Aladdin's magic lamp,' explained the boy. 'Do you perhaps know something about it, worthy one?'

A low laugh sounded in the cabin, followed by the words:

'No, my young friend, I know nothing about Aladdin's wonderful lamp. But I know a man who lives in southern Saoud, in the mountains. He would certainly have something to tell you.'

'I will go to find him,' decided Ali. 'What is his name?'

'His name is Baba. He lives as a Sufi—a hermit—in a cave. When he speaks, it is the truth.'

'I have more faith in his cave than in the Haoud-Kovvir of our magician who is now with the sharks.' Ali stretched lazily and asked: 'Why, O worthy one, are you going to Saoud?'

'Ten years ago,' answered the clear voice, 'I received a commission——'

'From the Shah-in-shah of Hindustan?' asked Ali.

'Yes, he sent me on this journey. I have, however, lost many years as prisoner of these pirates. Now at last I can go to Saoud to do that which I was commanded to do by my lord.'

'Ten years; that is a long time,' commented Ali. 'Would it not be better, worthy one, if we were to go direct from Basra to Hindustan?'

'What do you mean by that?'

'Like this,' breathed Ali, 'we can stop in Basra until there is a ship to Hindustan or a caravan is leaving for the passes. In the meantime I can ask the Sufi Baba in the cave about the magic lamp—then we go off; you, worthy one, Rahulo, your childish servant and I. When we are in Hindustan you can ask the Shah-in-shah——'

'—whether I can return to Basra to fulfil my task?' completed the voice of the old man. He laughed softly in the darkness and then said: 'Pay attention, young friend! If I tell you a story which no one apart from us two must know, will you promise not to repeat it to anyone?'

'My lips will be sealed more firmly than a grave!' said Ali.

On this assurance the voice continued to speak. Ali listened; and it is a fact that he did not speak about it to any man, at least not for a long time.

This, then, is what Whitebeard related in that dark cabin with the sound of the sea in the background.

'A little boy was born to the Shah-in-shah of Hindustan; a brown-skinned little Prince with great black eyes. His name was Ahmad.

'Rama Muni, the Grand Vizier, was an envious man. One night he stole the child, wrapped it in a bundle and gave it to a sea-captain who was journeying with his ship to distant lands. The Grand Vizier then returned to the palace thinking: When the Shah-in-shah dies I will mount his throne and not this little boy on whom to-morrow the fishes in the southern sea will be feeding.

'When the Shah-in-shah heard that his child had disappeared he tore his beard and sent out people to the four corners of the earth to find his little son and bring him back to Hindustan. For two long years they sought him but each one he had sent returned, shaking his head; for the Prince was nowhere to be found: not in Hong Kong, nor in Lhasa, nor in Peshawar.

'One day a young sailor appeared, returned home after a long voyage. He had heard that the Prince had been stolen two years previously. He now told the Shah-in-shah how the Grand Vizier had himself brought him a bundle and ordered him to cast it to the fishes. He had, however, untied the bundle and found in it a little boy, sleeping. Out of pity he had cared for the child throughout the voyage and finally, in Basra, given it to a woman who lived near the harbour.

'The good man then, naturally, feared for his head, but the Shah-in-shah rewarded him richly and commanded him to return with his ship to Basra. Me he charged to accompany the sailor in order to look for Prince Ahmad in Saoud, either in Basra or Bagdad; for he was convinced that the child in question had been the future Lord of Hindustan, his very own son.

'In the meantime Rama Muni, the Grand Vizier, had heard what the sailor related. He therefore escaped out of the palace before the guards could lay hands on him. Horsemen were sent after him, it is true, but he crossed the broad River Ganges and fled through the mountains into China.

'I had sailed with the loyal captain and it was on this journey that we were attacked by the pirates of the red moon. They killed everyone except me and my servant Rahulo, who lost his mind in consequence of these events. They kept us prisoners on the barren island of Mullak and demanded ransom from the Shah-in-shah. As soon as they received it they demanded twice as much—for ten long years I was used as their slave. But now I am continuing my journey to Basra to search for the heir to the throne of Hindustan——'

Ali breathed deeply and said:

'What, worthy one, if Ahmad has already been found? Who can know?'

'He has not been found!' answered the old man out of the darkness. 'A short while ago the man of the red moon dragged an Indian sailor to Mullak. This man told me many things before they killed him, only seven days before Sindbad anchored this ship off the island.'

'Allah!' gasped Ali. 'But how will you recognize Ahmad—even if you find him—after all this time? There are many young boys in Saoud with brown skins and black eyes. Perhaps he has been dead for a long time.'

'Prince Ahmad lives,' answered the clear voice. 'Whoever is born Prince of Hindustan does not die until he has inherited his Kingdom and lived his life in his native land.'

'How then will you recognize him, worthy one?' insisted the little beggar, drawing a deep breath; for he felt pity for the homeless Ahmad and a hot hatred against Rama Muni, the cruel Grand Vizier. Receiving no answer, Ali pressed:

'He will have grown up amongst strangers and will not know that his father is Lord of Hindustan and that he, himself, is a Prince of the East.'

'You have a wise little head, young friend,' said the old man. 'Let us now rest. It will soon be morning. Remember, however, that every Prince of Hindustan, when he has grown to dignity, bears the sign of it.'

'A sign?' asked Ali. 'What sort of a sign? What does it look like? Tell me, worthy one, so that I can help you search. You must know that I am quite clever when it is a question of looking for hidden things.'

'Also when they are magic lamps?' questioned the old man.

The lad did not enter into the joke and cried:

'What kind of a sign is it, worthy one?'

'The sign of a Prince in this world is remarkable,' said the old man. 'Not everyone can recognize it.'

'Could I see it?' Ali wanted to know.

'No, young friend—' was the thoughtful answer '—not so long as you are busy looking for the magic lamp to fulfil every wish—*your* wishes.'

'Who can see it, worthy one?' said Ali in a small voice.

'Loyal men,' continued the old man, 'naturally born leaders, not those who are kings merely through right of birth.' His voice seemed suddenly to tire. 'The very poor, who cannot even call their skins their own. Wise men who do not care about appearances or fashions. Artists who forget themselves, that their work may live. And the very old, who desire nothing more from life than death. All these can recognize the sign.'

'What would they see if they caught sight of it?' inquired Ali.

'It is like a diamond on the forehead, between the eyes, of him who bears it. It is like a ruby or like an emerald. Perhaps, also, it may be a brilliant light, which strikes the beholder's heart and makes him happy.'

Ali heard the old man sigh. He got up quickly from Sindbad's bed and said:

'I cannot understand your words, O worthy one, but I will help you look. Now you are tired and wish to rest. Forgive me, that I did not think of it before.' He, himself, was now wide awake.

'I am not tired but full of care,' replied the old man. 'Prince Ahmad is still far from home this night.'

The lad already stood at the doorway; he was about to

say something but, instead, shook his head and left the gloomy cabin. When he reached the deck, mast and boom loomed up dark against a red bank of cloud lying to eastward. Ali started as someone above his head began to laugh out loud.

Sindbad stood on the poop. His outstretched arm described a semi-circle around the horizon; from north to west and then over to south. 'No sail to be seen far and wide,' said Sindbad, laughing once more. 'I have left them behind me, those dogs of the blood-red moon!'

The cabin-boy shivered a little; he winked and thought: *I* have left them behind—*I!* How can he talk like that?

At that moment Sindbad called out: 'My ship is faster than all the pirates in the world!'

Grinning, Ali said: 'And you are the greatest sea-captain, great Sindbad.' To himself he was thinking: Sindbad was pale with fear when Whitebeard ordered him to turn the ship round in the storm.

The sailor bent over the rail and shouted:

'All hands of this watch stand by! Stand by, Ibrahim! Bear on the tiller and keep my ship going north—north, always north!'

It was time for the morning prayer; up crept the believers through the hatch from the hold, like beetles out of a hollow tree. And Sindbad, their lord and master, cried three times in a ringing voice:

'*Allahu akbar!*'

The morning was as bright and hot as any since Ali sailed in Sindbad's dhow. At midday a pitiless sun burned down over the waters. A dazzling blue from horizon to horizon. The sail, where the light caught it, blinded one's eyes. Even in the shade the planks were hot under the soles of the sailors' feet. Black bubbles and sticky drops oozed from between the boards. The sides of the ship smelt strongly of pitch.

And yet, a peaceful voyage after a stormy night! The wind died down. Shortly after midday the *Prince Omar* met with a current that gently carried her northwards.

No strange sail was anywhere to be seen. There was nothing but sea and more sea and a splendid expanse of blue sky. The higher one looked the paler became the blue; above the mast was a white field from whence the sun glared down.

'Little friend, light of my eyes,' said Sindbad, 'what are you going to do when this voyage is over? You haven't found the magic lamp?'

'Not yet,' corrected Ali. He squatted at the foot of the ladder and chewed on a date, as hard as leather. 'I think I shall go up to the mountains to ask a Sufi.'

'What use is a Sufi's information when Abu Bekr said the lamp was hidden on the island of Qalah?' Sindbad laughed ill-humouredly.

'It may be he can tell me how to steer in order to find the island,' said Ali lazily.

The sea-captain swallowed the gibe and said: 'Come with me, little friend, light of my eyes. That is much better. In Basra I take in freight for Bagdad; as soon as it is discharged I and my crew will set sail again. I shall find Qalah. Will you come with me?'

'As cabin-boy?' asked Ali. He shut his eyes and spat out the date-stone into what remained of the wind. He thought of the wizard's warning and grinned.

'As my cabin-boy, yes!' said Sindbad. 'On top of that you will get your full share of the cargo. We shall bring coconuts from Ceylon to Persia. Afterwards carpets from

Persia to Saoud! You will earn great sums of money and, with the help of Allah, you will see the island.'

'First I want to ask the Sufi,' countered Ali obstinately.

'Our friend will accompany me in future, my son,' said a deep and clear voice.

Ali and Sindbad turned their heads. The old man was standing in the opening of the cabin; his forehead in the shadow, his beard shining like threads of silver in the light.

'You are going with him?' asked Sindbad, surprised.

'Yes,' nodded Ali, 'I am going with this worthy one, great captain, to a far-distant land.'

The lad closed both eyes again and thought: Hindustan! He paid no further attention to what the two men were saying. An inner ecstasy held him in its grip, as one asleep, dreaming, who knows that he dreams in his sleep.

In the cool of the evening the wind freshened. Ali sat on the poop at the feet of the old man. He told Whitebeard in great detail the story of his life: that short story filled with so many high adventures, which only a beggar-boy, in those days, could experience. The old man nodded from time to time, kept silent but smiled a great deal. Nearby, Rahulo with his fat paunch lay on his back, gazing in wonder, like a child, at the great stars beginning to twinkle in the southern night sky. And once more Whitebeard nodded and smiled—but this was many days later. They were standing on the quayside. In Basra!

Ali said: 'Why can't I stay here? And how, worthy one, shall I find you when you come to Bagdad? The City of Happiness swarms night and day with people.'

Over from the ship came a shout. The dhow was lying alongside a mole jutting out from the quay. Sindbad stood aft, waving impatiently. The creaking of the tackle wafted across the water as the sailors hoisted the sail and hauled in the anchor.

'I shall come to Bagdad,' said the old man, 'when my business here in Basra is finished. In the meantime go and find the Sufi, if you can. Me you will find at the right time if you let your understanding and your inner voice guide you.'

Tall and gaunt, he stood on the river-bank as the brown-skinned cabin-boy climbed up the rope-ladder on board. Whilst the *Prince Omar* steered her way through the masts and spars and sailors' cries out into the Schatt al Arab, Ali waved his arms and cried:

'Come to Bagdad—soon!'

Now Whitebeard disappeared from sight. The distance between ship and river bank had become greater and greater. Then the cabin-boy felt a lump in his throat and swallowed. He felt now quite alone—lost in a strange world and as homeless as that Prince Ahmad from Hindustan, about whom he had heard.

It lasted only a moment. Sindbad came along and chased the boy up the mast. Up there he spent half the time of the voyage along the ancient waterway from Basra to Bagdad.

VIII

Behold—it is the City of Bagdad!

✦ ✦

LOOK out over a thousand roofs! Bagdad lies bathed
in the rising sun. Between cupolas and slender minarets the river flashes in the morning light—the River
Tigris. Southwards it flows—southwards to where the red
dust-storms blow. There where Basra lies, the port and the
sea. Those long streaks by the river banks are palm-groves,
with ripening dates. The trees rustle gently in the breeze
as it strokes their spreading tops.

A ship is coming up from the sea. The dark bow cleaves
the water of the Tigris in a foaming wave. The sailors stand
clinging to the rigging and start to sing when they catch
sight of Bagdad's towers. The triangular sail stands out in
contrast against the red brick walls; but whiter still are the
shining palaces on the river bank.

That man on the ship—red turban and blue trousers—
that is Sindbad the sailor. Hear his stentorian cry! He
throws his arms in the air and then sinks down on his
knees; he is offering up thanks to Allah, the Creator of the
Universe, who has brought him back safely through the
stormy seas to Bagdad—him and his ship.

See the fine houses of the rich with their shady court-
yards where cool fountains play!

And the crumbling walls of red clay where the poor are
sheltered.

And the grey clouds of dust round the booths in the
bazaar where flies encircle the Turkish honey.

Bagdad! The City of Happiness on the west bank of the Tigris. City of the Caliph, Haroun al-Raschid, the Just; the scene of his legends and adventures.

And the first person that Ali met as he came ashore in this wonderful city was—Hassan.

'Hi!' bawled the shaven-headed potter's son. 'Ali the thief is again in the land!' He hopped from one foot to the other and clapped his hands.

'Your father fished mud from the Tigris!' called out Ali in reply. 'Had you forgotten that, Hassan?'

The tall youth avoided a crowd of chattering Christians and, striding up, threatened: 'Now I will beat you black and blue, son of a thief!'

Up to now Ali had always run away. This time Hassan did not expect anything else. Moreover, half a dozen of his friends from the bazaar had turned up; so he opened his mouth wide and swore at the top of his voice.

The angry lout had forgotten that he had before him, not Ali the thief, but Ali the cabin-boy who was returning home after a long and dangerous voyage. Hard work and sea air had greatly strengthened the brown lad. And had Ali not knocked out a wizard? Had he not, in a raging storm, set fire to a pirate ship? Ha! Hassan could not know about that. That was why he found himself lying on his back before he could lay a finger on the hated little beggar.

Ali did not loosen his grip on his enemy's throat until Hassan's companions came up. They were a screaming gang of dirty hooligans, with coarse manners and venomous tongues. They fell on Ali's back like a pack of mongrel curs.

The little lad fought madly, using hands and feet and even his teeth, but it was not much good, for they were seven to one. But suddenly there was a respite in this whirl of fists and cries. Left and right the louts made off, bent double and sprawling away as fast as they could, whining and spitting the dust from their mouths.

Ali staggered to his feet, wiping the sweat and blood from his face. In front of him stood Ibrahim, the helmsman of the *Prince Omar*, and behind him a handful of his shipmates.

Ibrahim shook his head and was about to say something but did not get so far. With a clatter of hooves two horses dashed up. Men cried out and women-slaves screamed in the street. A sailor said:

'Look out! Djaffah's horsemen!'

At that very moment Ali felt a tug at his neck; he was caught by a leather thong. The black cloth of a burnous stroked his face. When he raised his head, two evil little eyes were staring down at him and a stern voice from the saddle demanded:

'Are you Ali, young dog?'

From a safe distance Hassan screamed: 'That's him! Ali! Keep hold of him! Ali the thief!'

Ibrahim and the sailors had moved away from the plunging horses and stood with their arms by their sides, not knowing what to do. A large crowd gathered round, for in those days the citizens of Bagdad were just as inquisitive as the street folk. Then a voice was heard:

'Ho! Horsemen! What are you doing there?'

The black turbans turned quickly round; two pairs of eyes glared threateningly at Sindbad as the sailor pushed a way through the spectators. 'Don't you know me?' cried the tall sea-captain. 'I am Sindbad! You have got my cabin-boy there. Let him go! At once! Otherwise, by Allah!—there will be trouble for you!'

All of a sudden a deathly silence reigned in the stifling square. Men and women stood mute with astonishment in the blazing sunshine; for no man in Bagdad had ever dared thus to address Djaffah's horsemen.

Ali thought: now they will take him along too! The leather sling threatened to throttle him.

'Let him go!' roared Sindbad. He planted himself, with legs astraddle, between the horses. 'I am just on my way to Haroun al-Raschid—may the sun of Heaven shine upon him! Must I tell the Ruler of the Faithful that Djaffah's horsemen have mishandled a friend of mine before my eyes? Must I say so—well?'

'This young dog is Ali the thief,' retorted one of the horsemen in a rasping voice. He pulled at the leather thong so that the lad's head bumped against his bent knee.

'O wise horsemen of Djaffah!' cried Sindbad. 'To-morrow the red executioner will be swinging his axe over two heads that are today wearing black turbans! Let Ali go!'

'Your threats are in vain!' came the answers. 'Out of the way! Djaffah's order is: Arrest them! Off with their heads! And that applies to this young dog in my sling. He broke into the house of the great Abu Bekr.'

Ali received a kick in the back. 'Run, thief!' came the harsh command from the saddle. The second horseman added: 'You are going to execution. Run!'

Ali had to run between the two horses and did not dare to stumble as the sling would have strangled him. His head buzzed and red spots danced before his eyes. Only in his ear was there a little hope left, for Sindbad had called after him:

'Courage, little friend! I am going to Haroun and will shortly save you.'

'He is known throughout the town as a windbag, this Sindbad,' said one of the horsemen. The other gave a mocking laugh.

For his part Ali could find nothing to laugh at. His arms and legs hurt him and the breath came bursting from his breast.

In this manner the horsemen dragged Ali through streets and squares swarming with people. Every now and then they beat him and made fun of his fear. When they had reached the high wall surrounding Djaffah's palace, they reined in their horses. As every child in Bagdad knew, this wall enclosed not only the magnificent house of Djaffah and the barracks for his soldiers. The prisons also lay on the other side of those loop-holes, behind which watching archers could be seen at any time of the day or night. Towards the river was a small gateway, narrow and heavily guarded. It was known as 'the Gate of Lost Souls'. Whoever was dragged through this gateway disappeared for ever into the bowels of the earth, into deep dungeons where the prisoners lay in chains. Should one of them ever see the light of day again, it was on the day when, in the great market place, the executioner swung his axe through the air.

A command was shouted. The narrow gate in the wall of the fortress swung open.

Now, Ali thought, I am lost!

He whimpered a little as the guards laid hold of him. Cursing him, they pushed him along a gloomy passage leading under the ground.

They came to a dungeon where Ali was seized by a big, powerful man. It was the torture chamber. Two shaggy attendants threw the lad down on a plank. The hefty jailer pressed an iron ring round his right ankle. To this was attached an iron chain with a round stone, as big as Ali's head, at the other end of it.

The prisoner had to carry chain and stone as the four of them passed through a black hole in the wall and then along another passage under musty archways and down slippery steps.

Now I shall never be able to ask the Sufi Baba about the magic lamp, thought Ali. He hobbled along with difficulty; the chain rattled, the stone knocked against his right knee at every step. His shadow danced ahead of him on the brick walls; the jailer's men were carrying torches from which the smoke brought tears to Ali's eyes.

Round a bend the little prisoner stumbled against some iron bars fixed across the passage. Foul air and a dreadful stench rose up to meet him. He stumbled backwards. A key-ring rattled, followed by the creaking of rusty hinges.

Ali was struck on the naked back by a clenched fist. He

fell forward and let go of the chain. Then he rolled steeply downwards and could feel damp clay between his fingers. The round stone on the chain rolled after him. So this, he was still able to think, is the prison under the earth. Then the stone struck his head and robbed him of all consciousness.

Whether beggar, cabin-boy or thief—it was all the same. After such a crack on the skull nothing matters very much. If one is lucky enough to come to again, it is difficult to collect one's thoughts.

So it was with Ali. When he opened his eyes, all around him was pitch-black night. The ground under his back was damp and cold. Mysterious sounds reached his ears.

He made a movement. The chain at his foot rattled; the iron ring scraped skin off his ankle. He lay still and listened.

The air stank of rottenness. Clanging noises and the murmur of voices came out of the darkness. From some way off came a whimper which ceased suddenly. Then a sharp cry, long drawn out. Nearer at hand began a hoarse sobbing which, it seemed, would never end. If you held your breath, you could hear a man begging for water in a toneless voice, over and over again.

Ali felt his hair rising. He shivered all over with cold and fear. Supporting himself on his shaking arms, he raised himself up. In this position he stared into the horrible night which shut him in so completely. Invisible to him, life was going on around; it crept and dragged itself here and there, many-footed, groaning, clinking with chains and iron fetters.

The boy uttered a cry and clapped his hands to his ears; he realized now only too well where he had landed.

The next moment an icy fear gripped him. Cold fingers

were feeling down his back. He quickly tried to move away but his fetters prevented him. Then a strong hand seized him by the arm. A voice said:

'Do not be afraid, my friend!'

Ali listened.

'You are alive!' said the unknown. 'That is good!' He removed his hand from the lad's arm. At that his fear left him and Ali gasped: 'Who are you?'

'A prisoner in this underworld!' came the answer.

Ali felt a thrill. Whoever it was spoke these words, he was certainly not from Saoud. The invisible voice sounded foreign and—yes—that was it! It reminded him of the speech of the old man with the white beard.

'I saw the torches up there behind the grille,' went on the unknown. 'I came along here after they had thrown you down. I thought at first that your neck was broken.'

'Oh, no!' said Ali cheerfully. 'Praise be to Allah! Not that! But it is cold here and this iron ring hurts my foot. Are you from Hindustan?'

'Yes,' came the clear answer. 'You have already noticed that?'

'You speak in the same fashion as my master. He is a much-honoured ambassador from Hindustan. I, Ali, am in his service!' explained the boy proudly, almost forgetting the chain and the fetter around his ankle.

'Servant of an ambassador from Hindustan?' came softly out of the darkness.

'Yes, yes!' Ali nodded vigorously, although no one could see him. 'My master is a proper ambassador of the Shah-in-shah. We met on a desert island, you know. He had been kept prisoner there for ten years. Now he has gone to Basra; soon he will be coming to Bagdad and——'

136

'Will never see you again!' completed the stranger. 'You and I,' he added, 'we lie in a dungeon from which no living man will emerge, unless it be on the way to the scaffold.'

'So it is said in Bagdad,' said Ali. He suddenly thought of Sindbad and went on quickly: 'I have a friend up in the town, a sailor—and he knows Haroun al-Raschid very well.'

'What use is his petition to the Caliph?' asked the stranger. 'These prisons are in Djaffah's power.'

'Every child knows that,' answered Ali slowly.

'And do you also know,' asked the other, 'that there is enmity between Djaffah and the Caliph, Haroun al-Raschid?'

'Everyone in Bagdad knows it,' admitted Ali.

There was a mocking laugh. 'Well then, if your good friend asks Haroun al-Raschid to have you freed, Djaffah will take care that you die before you leave these walls.'

'Do you really believe that?' asked Ali in a subdued voice. His hope was running out like sand through the fingers.

The answer came at once. 'If Haroun al-Raschid himself were to descend down here, then you might save your life, young friend. But no one in this terrible, endless night—not one of us—and there are hundreds—has ever heard of the Caliph coming here.'

Ali hung his head. The stranger, however, continued unperturbed:

'You were saying just now that your master from Hindustan spent ten years as a prisoner on an island?'

'Yes, I said so,' admitted Ali. 'His name is Asoka and his childish servant——'

'Stop!' cried the stranger sharply. He gripped the boy's shoulder. 'Asoka—did you say Asoka?'

'By Allah!' gasped Ali. 'That is his name. He is ambassador of the Shah-in-shah and is looking——' Ali stopped himself and bit his tongue so as not to give any more away.

'He is looking for Ahmad,' came out of the darkness. 'Ahmad who was stolen more than twelve years ago.'

'Yes, yes,' stuttered Ali. 'How do you know——'

'Sh—!' hissed the other. 'I, myself, am in the service of the Shah-in-shah. At his command I rode over the mountainous by-ways into Saoud. Here in Bagdad are men as true as gold. But before I could find them I was recognized by Rama Muni's hirelings; and Djaffah's horsemen arrested me. Now I lie here chained and my head must soon fall under the axe.'

'Has then this wicked Grand Vizier friends in the City of Happiness?' asked Ali in alarm.

'Rama Muni's friends,' was the answer, 'the associates of the disloyal Grand Vizier, are favourites of Djaffah. In the same way, all loyal men from Hindustan are Haroun al-Raschid's friends. There are thus two opposed camps in Bagdad. Whoever comes to the City of Happiness from Hindustan, whether by ship or riding on a camel, must belong to one or other of these two camps. There is war between these camps; secret war, fierce and cruel war with dagger, poison and treachery.'

'Allah!' cried the lad. 'I did not know that.'

'Rama Muni is recruiting mercenaries in China,' said the stranger, lowering his voice. 'His friends are seeking soldiers in Saoud and amongst the wild tribes in the hills. If the Shah-in-shah should die, the Princes will quarrel amongst themselves over the inheritance. That is what the

Grand Vizier is waiting for; that is the time he will choose to dash down from the mountains with his yellow horsemen. Then, woe to our land! There will be none to stop him. He will seize the crown of Hindustan!'

'But if Ahmad, the prince, is found, what then?' asked Ali excitedly.

'Ahmad—' came the reply softly. 'Yes—he, the prince, might be able to defeat Rama Muni. Ten thousand young men and all the rest of the people of Hindustan would follow him. He would only need to ride through the passes to his homeland. But where is Ahmad, the Prince of Hindustan?'

'Asoka of the white beard says that the Prince is living in Saoud; or perhaps in Basra, perhaps even in Bagdad,' said the lad, and then added: 'we must find him before Rama Muni comes with the Chinese—listen! What is all that?'

Voices could be heard approaching. A clamour surged up under the vault.

'Look! Torches!' said the stranger. 'They must be bringing new prisoners down here.'

Ali scarcely heard the words. He had noticed above, to one side, the red flicker of torches behind the black bars of the grating. By their dim smoky light the boy could see a crowd of ragged and emaciated figures, crouching to the left and right of him. Other figures appeared out of the black night, hobbling forward with piteous cries, wide-open eyes turned towards the faint light in the distance.

For the first time he could look into the face of his friend from Hindustan; a face with a stubbly beard, very thin, with a hooked nose and piercing dark eyes.

Then a chain rattled. Creaking, the grille was raised. A threatening voice roared:

'In the name of the Caliph, peace!'

The cries and whimpering ceased, like the surf on the sea-shore when the wind drops. And the man up there in the light of the torches cried:

'Haroun al-Raschid, the Just, Commander of the Faithful—the sun of Allah shine on his Glory! Haroun al-Raschid bids Ali, the beggar, cabin-boy and thief to come forth and show himself!'

'By all the gods!' gasped the Indian horseman, gripping the boy's arm. 'That means you!'

'What did I tell you?' grinned Ali. He turned his head and shouted at the top of his voice:

'Here I am. I am coming!'

'Try to find Ananda at the court of Haroun,' whispered the stubbly beard in his ear, and went on: 'say to him the Shah-in-shah has sent me. Tell him: Sar lies here in chains with his message!'

'That I will do,' nodded Ali, bending forward.

Dragging his chain and the stone with difficulty after him, he crept up the slippery incline towards the smouldering torches.

A pair of hands seized him. The grille fell rattling back into place whilst a wave of clamour broke out afresh from below. The two men from the torture-chamber laid the boy on the ground. With a few blows of his hammer the jailer knocked out the bolt from his fetters. He stood up, took a deep breath or two, and trotted away between the guards. Once again wild shadows danced on the brick walls ahead. Ali was then pushed through the low opening into the torture-chamber. His eyes opened wide with astonishment.

Men, standing in a semi-circle, filled the chamber. Distinguished-looking men! Soldiers of the palace guard in red cloaks were there and also Djaffah's horsemen in black burnous. Officers, with curved daggers encrusted with precious stones in their belts, and a big, tall nobleman was also there, taller than all the rest. He wore a dark green turban and a mouse-gray haik; a long brown beard covered his broad chest. And the name of this giant was—Haroun al-Raschid!

Ali threw himself on the ground before him. His forehead touched the paving-stones and his long hair brushed the tips of the Caliph's shoes.

'Stand up, my son!' said Haroun al-Raschid. 'Sindbad has told me of your courageous deeds on his voyage. You are a brave lad. I like the look of you, Ali!'

'Allah!' said the boy, but could bring no other sound from his throat. In his head, however, a hundred thoughts chased each other whilst he stood there in the torchlight before the Commander of the Faithful, dirty, dishevelled but shaking with pride.

'Two horsemen seized you early today,' went on the Caliph, 'and mishandled you. I heard this from Sindbad.'

'Yes—yes . . .' Ali bowed. He pressed his hands, as in confirmation, on his bare chest.

Haroun al-Raschid turned his head to one side and thundered: 'Both men shall be punished—forthwith!'

Ali followed the direction of his glance. He found himself looking into the face of a very lean man. A tremor shook his clay-encrusted legs. This lean man was Djaffah in person: black turban, black cloak, black eyes—Djaffah, the cruel! Djaffah, the merciless Sun of the Universe—as they called him in the City of Happiness.

A faint smile played round Djaffah's lips. He bowed his head slightly. When he spoke his voice sounded as hard as flint.

'They will be punished as you wish, O Caliph!'

Then, turning to those behind him, he commanded: 'Let all those horsemen who rode this morning approach!'

A young man left the chamber. Ali gave a start, for now Djaffah's eyes and Djaffah's voice were directed at him with the question: 'Two of my horsemen?'

'Yes, O Djaffah—two——' stuttered Ali. The torchlight reflected in Djaffah's eyes alarmed him.

'Let us go!' said Haroun al-Raschid.

So it came about that Ali, the beggar-boy, walked in the company of the All-Highest down long passages and under narrow archways. His heart beat as quickly as that of a frightened bird. At last they came to a great hall and passed out through two pillars into a wide courtyard, surrounded on all sides by the walls of the fortress. Djaffah stepped forward and said:

'These, O Caliph, are my soldiers who rode in the morning watch!'

He waved his outstretched arm from left to right over the whole breadth of the courtyard which sweltered under the burning sun.

Ali stood with Haroun al-Raschid in the shade of an archway. He caught the mocking smile on Djaffah's face as he ordered.

'Two of my horsemen! Show them to me, young beggar! Even if you can only point out one of them, I will believe you!'

Thirty paces in front, motionless in the dazzling light, a squadron of horsemen was drawn up across the yellow sand. Fifty black horses, each one the counterpart of the other! Fifty men in their saddles, each one muffled in a black burnous!

'If he cannot find them he must return, as a proved liar, whence he came.'

Turning to Ali, he commanded harshly: 'Go! Show me the man who caught you in his sling!'

Ali said: 'Supposing I can point out the horsemen, what then, great Djaffah?' He took a step forward. Now he was again in the sunshine he could feel the life returning to his limbs, which had grown cold and stiff under the ground. Also he did not mind how much Djaffah, by way of answer, knit his brows darkly.

'The lad speaks sense,' broke in the Caliph. 'If he is to be punished if he has lied—he and his friend Sindbad—then it is only just that he should be rewarded if he has spoken the truth. Find the man who caught you and a wish of yours shall be granted.'

'Show us this man, then!' said Djaffah, the mischievous smile again on his lips.

The great Djaffah believed, in fact, that no one could pick out one soldier from a whole crowd, for his horsemen resembled one another like so many eggs. What the people in the streets of Bagdad managed to see of these men was no more than brown, clutching hands and a pair of eyes to go with them. Not one of them showed his face; they wore black turbans and black scarves around the lower part of the face.

'Go—look!' hissed Djaffah venomously through his white teeth.

'Let the horsemen dismount, O Djaffah,' said Ali.

The merciless 'Sun of the Universe' gave a signal with his head. Hereupon an officer stepped forward and gave a short word of command. There was a rustling of black burnous. Horses snorted and pawed the ground; curving scimitars clanked. Fifty riders in black cloaks stood with crossed arms in front of their horses.

Ali hesitated, took one step forward, then another, and

finally walked across the hot sand to the right-hand end of
the line of soldiers. Here, in front of the first man, he stood
on his toes, in order to look into the eyes which glared at
him angrily from over the black scarf.

It did not take long. The lad sighed and side-stepped
towards the second soldier. He was taller than the first and
Ali had to crane his neck as high as possible.

144

He reached the third horseman and the fourth—sixth, seventh, eighth, ninth, tenth. He looked carefully at them all and not one of them made a movement. Every time Ali stood on his toes, he got an angry look from a pair of dark eyes.

He had already sampled twenty-four such pairs of eyes. He was now in the centre of the rank and had not found any clue. Over in the shade by the walls he heard voices; they were arguing whether the half-naked beggar was a liar or not—and Sindbad as well—but Ali did not worry much about that.

The next moment a shrill cry rent the air over the hot courtyard. The spectators, in spite of the glaring sunshine, stepped forth from the shade, all together: Haroun al-Raschid, the Caliph; Djaffah and all the officers and guards.

Ali was pulling at a black haik and crying: 'Here he is! This was the man—this one here!'

With hatred in them, the narrow eyes of the soldier stared down at him.

'Did you capture this boy today?' asked Djaffah threateningly, as he pointed to the little beggar.

'Yes,' came the muffled reply from behind the black scarf.

Haroun al-Raschid gave a nod of recognition. The other lords said 'Ah!' They also said 'Oh!' for they were very astonished.

'Who rode with you?' hissed Djaffah.

'Halef ben Husain,' answered the horseman.

Djaffah turned to a tall officer. 'Cast them both in chains!' he commanded.

In a twinkling six horsemen in red mantles dashed across the sweltering courtyard. Whilst the two soldiers were being taken away, the remainder of Djaffah's black riders rode off in formation on their fine, glossy horses.

'This young beggar must be in league with Shaitan!' said Djaffah furiously.

'He is certainly clever,' nodded the Caliph. His brown fingers stroked the long beard. Everyone could see that he did not grudge Djaffah, his secret enemy, this defeat.

Ali fidgeted and asked: 'May I now have my wish, lord?'

'Speak up!' laughed the Caliph. 'Your wish will be fulfilled.'

'At once?' Ali wanted to know. He danced from one leg to the other.

'At once!' smiled Haroun al-Raschid.

Ali drew a deep breath and said: 'Down there in the dungeon lies a horseman from Hindustan. He is my friend. Command, O great Caliph, that he be released.'

'A horseman from Hindustan?' asked Haroun al-Raschid, surprised. He looked inquiringly into Djaffah's face.

'Yes,' said Ali quickly, 'his name is Sar. He is a messenger of the Shah-in-shah of Hindustan. He is asking for Ananda, a man at your court, lord. But he is at present attached to a chain under the ground.'

'Free this man instantly and bring him to me!' cried the Caliph. Ali noticed the veins in his neck were swollen with anger.

'As you wish, O Caliph,' said Djaffah. He shot a look of hatred at the lad who had given away this secret.

'Come with me, little friend,' said Haroun al-Raschid. 'You are free now.'

And so it happened that Ali, the brown-skinned beggar, at the side of the Commander of the Faithful, passed through the narrow gateway, out from Djaffah's fortress.

Surrounding them was a chattering host of magnificent, rich and remarkably distinguished lords.

'One thing I should like to know,' said the Caliph on the way. 'How did you recognize Djaffah's horseman?'

'Oh,' grinned Ali, 'that was simple! When this man caught me in his sling this morning I noticed his eyes. He had no eye-lashes; his eyelids were red from the dust. And just under his left eyebrow was a scar. A thin scar, made, I should think, with a knife.'

At this the fine gentlemen murmured amongst themselves, praising the youth's cleverness and nodding their recognition at him; and the Caliph said:

'You have your wits about you, my young friend. I now believe everything Sindbad has told me!'

Three gold coins clinked into the beggar-boy's brown hand.

IX

◆ ◆

SOME hours later Ali had related the story of his voyage down to the smallest detail.

His grandmother only nodded. The shadow of her skinny head fluttered on the bare wall. In a faltering voice she then said: 'Allah be praised! You did nothing foolish on your voyage.' The toothless mouth closed in a tight line. She sat bent forward, looking at the sooty flame shed by the old, dented lamp.

'Nothing foolish!' growled Ali. He had expected praise! Excitedly he had told everything, everything! Starting with his sea-sickness right down to his imprisonment in the dreadful dungeon under the earth!

'Nothing foolish!' he mocked, and brought out a handful of coins from his red loin-cloth. He jangled them a little in his hands, letting the light play on the bright discs. 'This—here—' he insisted. 'What about this?'

He felt a mischievous enjoyment as the old woman stared in wonder at the pile of money in his hands.

'Seven years,' said the rascal, 'no—ten years you could beg at the Gate of the Prophet and not get half as much!' He closed his hands, shook them and then opening them again, said proudly:

'Not a single one of them is stolen! These three—as new as a day-old chick—they were given me by the Caliph, Haroun al-Raschid, may Allah protect him! The others I

148

got from Sindbad the sailor because I knocked down the magician and set the red pirates' ship on fire. An dthese coins here—' he pushed them forward with his thumb, '—these beautiful coins were given me by the Whitebeard from Hindustan, because I am now his servant. A month's wages! Is all that perhaps nothing, Grandmother?'

The old woman sighed and shook her head. 'Don't be too proud of your good luck,' she warned him cautiously. 'Don't grow proud, my grandson.'

On top of all that, thought Ali, there is all the business of Ahmad. He had not said a word about this. That was a secret—Ahmad Prince of Hindustan. He thought a moment, then leaned forward and laid the coins solemnly in the ragged lap of the beggar-woman.

'I will make you a present of them, Grandmother,' he said slowly.

She could not believe her ears. Before her half-blind eyes the shining gold twinkled in the lamp-light. Tremblingly the withered hands fingered the unexpected riches.

'Buy yourself a dress!' cried Ali. 'Sandals! A turban! And bread and fruit every day!' He ran his hands through his long hair, brushing it back over his ears. 'I shall get more of these—' he pointed to the coins '—as soon as I get the magic lamp.'

'Ah! You did not find it on this voyage,' chuckled the old woman. She was swaying backwards and forwards with pleasure. Never had she believed in such things as miracles and magic lamps; these were but fairy stories for children and fools, and perhaps, who could tell, Ali her grandson, was a half-wit . . .

'Let us sleep now,' she said and snuffed out the burning wick in the lamp.

The boy groped his way in the dark to his bed of rags.

He lay there listening to the quick breathing of his grandmother over by the wall. Now and then she murmured something incomprehensible; sometimes there was a whistle in her breathing, like mice scuttling.

Behind the door-rag the street was still. The little beggar lay awake on his back. With open eyes he looked out into the darkness, thinking of the wonderful lamp which could fulfil all his wishes, thinking of Ahmad, the homeless king's son. Ahmad! Heir to a kingdom full of all magnificence and now lost in a foreign land, with no name, unknown. 'Protect him, Allah!' whispered Ali. 'Protect him and succour him wherever he may be; save Ahmad from his enemies and bring him safely home to Hindustan.'

So Ali fell asleep. But it was no deep, peaceful sleep. On the contrary. Scraps of dreams floated through his brain. And in his dream Ali stood on a high mountain. Down in the valley he saw a boy who was asleep. Horsemen in black mantles approached and the horses threw up so much dust that the sun disappeared behind a cloud. Black riders—Djaffah's horsemen! Yet they were not; for they had yellow hands, yellow faces. They were Rama Muni's horsemen—his Mongolian soldiers. They were searching for Ahmad who slept under a tree in the valley.

Ali wanted to shriek. But no sound came from his mouth. He could hear the thunder of horses' hooves over the hard ground; and the brown lad went on sleeping, sleeping—and the horsemen were already at hand.

He gasped and turned over. Right in his ear a voice whispered:

'Wake up, little friend!'

A hand shook him by the shoulder at which he opened his eyes, catching his breath.

'Wake up. Get up—you must fly——'

'Zainab?' said Ali in surprise, recognizing the water-carrier's voice.

'Quick!' said the young man; Ali felt his breath on his forehead. 'Djaffah's soldiers are dragging the people from their beds and asking where you are.'

'I was dreaming of savage horsemen . . .' murmured Ali.

'Who is that?' asked the faltering voice of the old woman. Her hurried breathing could be heard in the dark; and now another sound struck the boy's ears: the clatter of hooves!

'The fifty horsemen are out!' said the water-carrier. 'The whole city is in an uproar. They have stationed men everywhere. Horsemen patrol all the streets. Get up and run for your life, little friend!'

Ali lay stiff on his bed of rags. He held his breath and listened; the sound of the hooves came nearer.

'I must go,' whispered the water-carrier. 'Be quick, little friend, or you are lost!' His hand fell away from the lad's shoulder. As the door-cloth was pushed aside, Ali saw that it was already dawn.

He got up suddenly and slipped by the ragged carpet. He peered carefully in both directions. A stretch of the alley between the narrow walls was lit by the early morning light. Each way, the corner of a house obstructed the view. A horse snorted quite close by. Ali crouched quivering in the doorway. When the horseman came in sight Ali was up and away.

In a few bounds he was round the next corner. He leaped back. The end of the alley was blocked by black riders on black horses. One of them threw both arms in the air and shouted a command. The chase began. Cries and the beat of horses' hooves came from all directions.

Ali flung himself against a door which happened to be near him. Allah be praised! The wood was rotten and the bolt on the inside gave way. Ali fell head over heels into a dimly-lit room. Just beside him a bearded fellow jumped out of his bed and began to bellow. In front of the door were already neighs, curses and the rattle of sabres.

He found a ladder in one corner. Nimble as a monkey, Ali clambered up through the strange house. At the top he pushed with his head against a trap-door and threw it open. He then slid on his stomach out on to the flat roof, just as a guard gripped the ladder and panted after him.

Ali did not lose a second. To the right of him was an earthen jar. He seized the heavy vessel and pushed it down through the opening. The answer was a howl, curses, and a mighty banging to and fro.

Ali now made for the knee-high parapet which surrounded the roof. A jump landed him on to the next house which lay somewhat lower. It was no time for dallying. Straight across and, climbing this time, on to the next house, and so on! A nimble-footed lad could traverse a whole quarter of Bagdad on the roofs of the houses, jumping with safety over the narrow streets—in those days! There were no gables or tiles.

But Ali, as he ran, realized there must come an end, for Bagdad in those days was built in the form of a wheel. Radiating from the centre of the city, the bazaars divided the sea of houses into three parts. To reach one roof from another across the bazaar—that only the birds could do; but no little beggar, no cabin-boy and no thief!

Ali hid himself behind a parapet, like a hare hoping to throw the dogs off the scent. His breath came fast; the skin on his arms and legs was scratched and torn in a dozen places. The house, on the roof of which he crouched, was one of the tallest in this quarter so that he was able to keep a good look-out for his pursuers. Carefully he raised his head over the top of the parapet, and what he saw was not exactly comforting.

A dozen of the black guards were approaching him over the roofs. They waved and called to one another, and had the appearance of a flock of crows fluttering over a desert of grey cubes. The nearest of these birds of ill omen was so close that Ali could have raised a bump on his head with a stone.

The question is, thought Ali, whether this whole quarter of the city is watched by these vultures. There was only one hope. A very little one, to be sure, under the golden rays of the morning sun, rising out of Persia into the heavens; just a faint chance. And this merest glimmer of hope was—the Tigris!

He must reach the river at all costs. A run through the streets was useless, for Djaffah's soldiers rode swift horses. They could also climb. But whether they could swim as well as he, Ali, would have to be put to the proof!

He ran off, bent double and flopped on to the next roof. He no longer wasted time glancing round at his pursuers. He ran and climbed, and when he crossed over a street caught a glimpse below of a swarm of faces looking up from the shadowy gorge. Every leg in the whole quarter seemed to be after him.

At last, at his feet, the water flashed in the light. He began to clamber down quickly. Bricks and mortar broke off in his hands; dried clay fell in showers as the boy slithered down out of a cloud of dust into the street. He fell sprawling and rolled over and over.

Although Djaffah's horsemen uttered a shout of triumph, they arrived too late on the spot. They might spur their horses to the utmost but the little beggar was fleeter. From right under the pounding hooves of the horses the red loin-cloth fluttered away and dived over the river bank, deep down into the Tigris.

Ali swam under water with the current. He felt the blood hammering in his veins. When he came to the surface his face was only visible for a moment. But this was long enough for the black horsemen. With their shout in his ears, Ali dived again.

By means of strong strokes with arm and leg and the help of the current, Ali hoped to escape downstream. Under the water he kept his eyes open; his thoughts flashed quickly through his mind whilst all the time he swam like a fish. Of course! They would put out boats and row and row until they caught him.

Three times he came to the surface for air and took no notice of his pursuers. He did not turn to look, for this was a race—a race for his head. And he knew that Djaffah would not twice let him slip through his hands. Djaffah— the cruel Sun of the Universe—would say: 'Off with his

head!' and Haroun al-Raschid would never know about it.
The next time he surfaced he accidentally turned his
head. Up there was the bridge of boats connecting the
eastern with the western bank. Then Ali felt a shock of
fear. For on the bridge of boats trotted black horses, black
scarves fluttering in the breeze and spear-points sparkling
in the morning sun.

He dived in the knowledge that now Djaffah's horsemen
would be posted on the opposite shore. I am swimming,
thought Ali, straight into their arms, and yet . . .

There was still just one possibility! The gardens of the
rich. They lay behind those high walls, built right up to
the east bank of the Tigris. Even Djaffah's men would not
dare to intrude into those marvellous gardens, where the
wealthiest and noblest citizens of Bagdad allowed their
wives and daughters to stroll about.

His lungs were bursting. A few more strokes and he came
up again to the surface. He had hardly taken a breath when,
left and right, feathered arrows whistled past his ears and
splashed into the water.

Frightened, Ali dived down deeper than ever before,
until it was so dark he could only tell his direction by the
current. Now he changed his direction and came up for
air where he was not expected. His dripping mop of hair
had disappeared again below the little waves before the
archers could even take aim.

Two boats glided into the river, each manned by six
Negroes. At the bow of each vessel stood or kneeled one of
Djaffah's soldiers, in a black cloak and coal-black turban.
Each held an arrow ready in his bow-string.

The black head of the swimmer kept on bobbing up,
sometimes ahead of them and sometimes to their right
downstream. The boy changed direction surprisingly

swiftly; the archers were never able to take proper aim. Nevertheless, the arrows fired at random spurted up ever closer and closer.

The best swimmer, even in those days, could not swim as fast as a boat rowed by six strong arms. Ali lost his lead because, after every breath he took, he had to dive again. They soon caught him up and the moment arrived when his head appeared out of the water between the two boats; one downstream and one upstream from him. The men shouted and stopped rowing.

Now these black-hearted fishermen felt sure that the nimble fish would soon be wriggling in their hands. The ships veered and the Negroes pulled with all their strength to lessen the distance between them.

Ali's head bobbed up again but not where his fierce enemies expected him. He came up half an arrow-shot to their rear towards the middle of the Tigris. The archers could not shoot because the one boat was too far off and the other had turned.

This time Ali could really fill his lungs. Again he plunged and swam down to a great depth. Then he put into practice a little trick, taught him by a sailor who dived for pearls in far-off islands: he turned on his back under the water and swam thus with sideways movement of his arms, without any loss of depth. Taking great care, he waited until the blurred shadow of the boats approached and then let himself rise. It was high time; his lungs were bursting.

The cunning which Ali employed that night, after he had broken into Abu Bekr's house, succeeded again this time, in spite of the bright day shining over the Tigris. Djaffah's soldiers did not look for the runaway under the stern of their boats.

Ali heard the dip of the oars to his sides and the voices

of the men above him. At last he could rest a little and must only take care that his fingers had a grip of the hull. That was not so difficult; the vessel was a clumsy thing without any keel but with enough projecting planks under the water.

The soldiers cursed with astonishment. They just could not understand how the brown-skinned rascal could stay under water so long.

'He must be a young wizard!' cried one.

'He is a Djinn or is in league with Shaitan!'

Ali grinned and nearly spluttered. Then he heard a voice of authority say:

'Hodjy is beckoning—row faster. This young dog will *have* to come up some time for air! We will search the water between here and the bank.'

The bank! thought Ali. He must mean the eastern bank for the sun was aft of the boat. That was Ali's good fortune that morning, for his head was in the shadow of the sloping stern.

The vessel was more than half-way across the river and gradually approaching the opposite bank. Ali could see the second boat a good distance downstream, when he carefully poked his head to starboard. Upstream the bridge of boats looked like a dark beam across the Tigris. More boats put off from the bank and came towards them in a fan-like formation. A little farther off was the sail of a Sambuk, running in the morning breeze to Basra—perhaps to Africa —who could know? Ali wished longingly that he were standing on the dry deck of this ship with its sail flashing in the bright sunshine.

He again peeped through the poles of the rudder which sloped from the hull into the water. Ahead of them was a whitewashed wall rising straight out of the Tigris.

Some great man's park and garden must lie behind it. These gardens—every child knew it—were full of ponds and little lakes; somewhere at the foot of the wall there ought to be an opening, carrying the river-water into the park.

Suddenly the sunshine disappeared; the boat had reached the shadow of the wall. Ali took a great breath and dived, but he had not reckoned on the long shadows of the early morning.

He swam with strong swift strokes. There was no bank! He let the air out slowly through his nose. There was no bank! He must come up again.

A cry reached his ears as from a distance. He was discovered. Through a veil of dripping water he saw, just in front, the rough surface of the whitewashed wall. He dived. Five, six arrows hissed through the water exactly where his neck had been.

Under the water he searched about wildly. He could hear the splashing of the oars above his head. In front of him spread a dark barrier; a small fish flashed past his face; then his right hand struck against the soft mantle of plants that grew thickly at the foot of the wall. He let the current pull him slowly along until his head and breast were well-nigh bursting.

There was no opening; he must go up again for air. With a great effort he succeeded once again in rising up under the boat lying darkly on the bright surface. He could see the motionless oars, like the legs of a gigantic beetle, sticking out into the water.

However, he no longer felt safe at the stern. Greedily he drank the air into his tormented lungs and was suddenly aware that the long oars were being pushed towards him over the gunwale. He knew that they would be sure to

find him soon, but as he clung with his finger-tips to a wooden ledge he began to feel a wave of weakness and dizziness sweep over him. His blood sang in his ears and his legs up to his loins seemed to grow heavy and to be sinking.

When he was again able to dive, he knew it was for the last time. It was now a question either of finding the opening of the channel in the wall or of giving up the contest.

With his right hand he rummaged up to the elbow in the luxuriant underwater plants. Clouds of mud darkened the water and betrayed his position. He felt a sharp knock on the back of his hand; shortly afterwards his fingers closed round the shaft of an arrow, embedded in the thick growth.

Quite unexpectedly his arm pushed through the curtain of plants up to the shoulder. He worked forward with his head, the air bubbling from his mouth. His outspread fingers touched sand as well as mud; his back scraped against some slippery growth. With his last ounce of strength he fought through the narrow channel, pushing, pulling, until at last he struck against the wooden trellis that protected the opening.

He closed his eyes. This was the end of the struggle. He had no strength left to break through the trellis although it only consisted of saturated and rotten wood. There was no air left in his lungs; for that he must return to the Tigris. His body turned over. It was all like some frightful dream as his hands slid upwards away from the slippery stones . . . And then he found himself breathing through his open mouth. Astonished, he opened his eyes. There was nothing to see. It was pitch-dark dark; but there was air.

Ali gulped it down whilst his heart hammered against his ribs. And what air it was, too! An abominable, sweetish smell of decay, but at least one could fill the lungs with it and not suffocate and drown.

'Allah!' panted the lad; something, a fish or a rat, brushed cold against his neck, splashed about and made off.

He shut his eyes again and breathed long and deep until his heart beat somewhat less painfully. He then brushed his mud-plastered hair from his face and felt with his feet for the wooden trellis. When he had found it he quickly smashed the rotten wood and forced his way through. After a few strokes he was suddenly blinded by the sunlight. With some difficulty, he clambered up and found himself staggering through a pond, only knee deep. At the brink he let himself drop on to beautiful dry grass between bushes of green leaves with red flowers.

It was still fairly early in the morning.

Well—on the soft grass, between the flowering shrubs, under the red blossoms, Ali slept till midday.

At last he awoke and opened his eyes.

The first thing he noticed was a pair of small feet; they were standing so close to him on the green grass that he could have stretched out an arm and touched them. They were dainty, brown feet; but as the lad had been sleeping face downwards, he could see nothing else but the hem of some golden-yellow garment. He turned over slowly. His glance followed the folds of the rich, silken dress upwards into the green foliage. Above the leaves were flowers, deep red and sweetly smelling. And between these blooms, as big as his hand, Ali discovered a pair of round, dark eyes, steadily contemplating him.

The foliage rustled; a twig snapped. Surrounded with leaves and blossom, a face appeared—a brown face in which the big, dark eyes twinkled inquisitively, and a small voice, like the warbling of a bird, asked:

'Are you a Djinn?'

Ali grinned with relief. It was only a little maiden in the bushes! He shook his head and said:

'No, little sister, I am no Djinn.'

'But you have plants in your hair and your skin is like sand!' whispered the girl from out of the leaves.

'Ah! well,' nodded Ali, 'I have been swimming under the water through mud and sand and weeds.' He began to comb out his clammy hair with his fingers.

'No man may enter this garden alive!' said the girl.

'Haroun al-Raschid's guards watch it day and night. You must be a Djinn!'

'Very well then,' replied Ali, 'I *am* a Djinn.' The bit about the day and night guards made him think hard. To himself he said: If she thinks I am a spirit she will do what I want, otherwise she may easily betray me and then . . .

Here, in the Caliph's park, he was at any rate safe from Djaffah's horsemen, as long as he was not discovered by the guardians of the garden.

'You are the first Djinn I have ever seen,' said the brown maiden. 'What is your name?'

The question rather embarrassed Ali. He stroked his face and said:

'What do you think?'

'Oh . . .' the dark eyes in the foliage closed. The girl thought a little and then said:

'You cannot be Ebli's son Zulbazan—no! You are much too nice for him. Also you aren't Dulhan; he is invisible, so that he can disturb the faithful when they are at prayer in the mosque. Perhaps you are Muboot?'

'Do you mean Muboot who is such a terrible liar?' asked Ali.

The red flowers swayed about as the girl nodded her agreement.

'No,' grinned Ali, 'I am not Muboot, but he is a relative of mine. In the spirit world I am known as the Djinn of the lamp.'

'Djinn of the lamp—that is pretty!' decided the maiden. 'But why are you called that?'

'Because,' explained Ali, turning right over on to his back, 'because I have got to find a lamp which has been hidden somewhere in the world ever since the time of Solomon.'

164

'Ah!' said the girl. 'What kind of a lamp is it?'

'A magic lamp—Aladdin's wonderful lamp, you know!' The little brown head nodded so violently that the golden-yellow veil slipped from her black hair. 'I know about this magic lamp from the legend. You only have to rub it with your hand when a powerful Djinn appears and fulfils all your wishes. Do you think you will be able to find it?'

'Yes, why not?' answered Ali. He stretched his arms lazily behind his neck.

They both remained silent for a little while; the boy inert on his back in the grass, the inquistive maiden half hidden in the foliage. The air was heavy with scent and sunshine. Thousands of insects hummed their morning song. At length the little maid asked:

'Djinn of the lamp! Is it true that all spirits are the subjects of King Solomon?'

'Yes, yes,' answered Ali. 'Spirits, ghosts, ghouls and Djinns—all must obey him.'

'You, too?'

'Of course!'

'Is it true that the great King Solomon sealed up disobedient spirits in bottles and threw them in the sea?'

'Certainly,' replied Ali. 'I could tell you a story about that.'

'Oh, please, Djinn of the lamp, tell it to me!' The little brown face swayed with pleasure amongst the blossoms and the leaves.

'Well,' said Ali, 'it happened to some of my relations. I must tell you that most of my relations are not ghosts but just simple spirits—rather stupid spirits, in fact. In those days, when King Solomon lived on earth, they were just as silly as they are today, and terribly fond of gossiping.

They chattered about everything in the world—stupidities—of course. They were so hopelessly stupid that Solomon said: "I am going to put the whole lot in a bottle, seal up the neck and throw it into the sea, where it is deepest!" '

Ali grinned with amusement.

'And then?' asked the girl. 'Did he really seal them up and throw them in the sea?'

Ali shook his head. 'Unfortunately no!'

'Why not?'

'He forgot about it.'

'Why did he forget about it?' asked the girl, disappointed.

'Well, I will explain,' went on Ali. 'Pay attention, little sister. It happened like this. The bottle was all ready; the great and wise King Solomon blew out his cheeks and was just about to blow half my relations into the neck of the bottle when the Queen of Sheba came along to visit him. That gave him plenty to do and he forgot all about the spirits.'

'Ah!' said the little maid. 'The spirits must have been very glad.'

'Not in the slightest,' said Ali. 'They are much too stupid to be glad about anything!'

'What exactly are you doing here in the Caliph's garden, Djinn of the lamp?' the girl now wanted to know.

'Oh,' said Ali, 'I was bathing and having a little rest. I shall have to leave soon—in a couple of hours. And you also must go now, little sister, so that no one will know that a Djinn lies hidden here under the leaves. What is your name?'

'Fatima,' said the little maid softly.

'All right then,' said Ali. 'Now listen, Fatima! You must go and fetch me what I need: some blue silk for a turban, and some yellow cloth—and dates, plenty of dried dates! I am going to sleep. Place everything here under this bush. But no one must know anything about it. Do you understand?'

'Yes, no one!' whispered the girl. 'Afterwards, can I wish for something?'

Ali scratched his head and, after a moment, said: 'No, afterwards you must not speak another word. If you want to wish you must do it now.'

He felt embarrassed, for it was understood that whoever should give help to a Djinn, her wishes would be fulfilled. And how could he hope to fulfil any wish of this little maid? He scratched his ears.

Then the brown girl said solemnly: 'Dear Djinn of the lamp, I want the magic lamp.'

Ali grinned with relief and answered quickly: 'You can have it—but only when I find it!'

The foliage rustled, the branches swayed about, a red blossom fell to the ground. The little maid had gone.

'What a fool I am!' said Ali to himself; for it had just dawned on him that he had promised away Aladdin's lamp. Now, if he searched for it and found it, he would have to bring it along to this girl—but stop! A subtle thought occurred to him. He was no Djinn! He was merely Ali, the beggar-boy, who had only escaped by the skin of his teeth from Djaffah's rough soldiers.

'Allah be praised!' said Ali out loud. 'I am no Djinn—so there is no need for me to fulfil any wishes!'

He grinned with satisfaction and lay down again on his back. There in the shade he dozed away throughout the afternoon and was only aware of some faint rustlings amidst the gentle sounds of the garden. Later, he found some blue silk hidden under the green leaves, also a piece

167

of yellow cloth and a little bag filled with dates, almonds and other nice things.

The brown-skinned little sister has done more than I asked, he thought.

When evening came and night began to fall, Ali made a bundle of the things and disappeared under water out of the quiet garden.

X

From words take only what is true;
All deception then must end.
Everything to Good will tend—
Allah wisdom gives to you!

◆ ◆

AFTERNOON. At the edge of a little thicket Ali squatted on the carpet of dry weeds. With half-closed eyes he looked out of his shady nest and saw between gnarled tamarisks the heat shimmering over the land of Saoud. Afar off, the river gleamed here and there; but Bagdad, the City of Happiness, lay engulfed in the red and dusty mist of the day. Now and again a puff of wind struck the thicket and the dry foliage rustled; then, over Ali's back, flowed a wave of heat, the glow from the rocks which, behind the bushes and trees, pointed to heaven, red and yellow and barren.

He held his breath and listened—there it was! A faint sound, the tinkle of a small bell reached his ears.

Below, a shadow moved in the rocky defile. A donkey, with outstretched neck, appeared round a boulder. Behind this donkey came another and yet another pair of grey ears. Six donkeys in Indian file! At their rear stumped a little man with bandy legs and a bright red beard.

Ali grinned. He spat out a date-stone and slithered down through the shrubs into the defile.

The little man stopped in surprise whilst his donkeys continued on their way.

'Old friends in the mountains!' cried Ali. 'Have you come straight from the city, Ali Baba?'

The red-bearded wood-merchant swallowed hard and

the hairs on his chin trembled as he said: 'That must be Ali, the thief—or his ghost!' He passed his hand over his eyes. 'Didn't you drown in the Tigris, the day before yesterday?'

'Yes,' laughed Ali. 'The day before yesterday I led Djaffah's guards by the nose—but only just!'

'Everyone in Bagdad believes that you disappeared for ever in the river.' Ali Baba gave a giggle and rubbed his hands with pleasure.

'All the better,' said the lad. 'Is there any news from the City of Happiness?'

'Oh, great news, as a matter of fact, little friend!' said Ali Baba. He raised his thin eyebrows. 'An ambassador from Hindustan arrived yesterday. Bagdad is in such a turmoil——'

'A tall man with a silvery beard?' asked Ali.

'Yes, by Allah! You know that?' The wood-merchant was surprised. With a solemn gesture he went on: 'The Prince of Hindustan will make an appearance . . .'

'When?' asked Ali, gripping the man's arm.

'Tomorrow—the day after tomorrow! So the ambassador from Hindustan said. Haroun al-Raschid, our Caliph —Allah protect him!—Haroun al-Raschid had it proclaimed in all the bazaars by Djaffah's horsemen. Now Bagdad is swarming like an ant-heap. All are awaiting Ahmad of Hindustan.'

'Is he coming from Basra?'

Ali Baba shook his head and said in an aggrieved voice: 'That's just the trouble. Nobody knows from what direction the Prince will come. Haroun al-Raschid—the sun of Allah shine upon him!—has had all the gates of the city decorated with silken flags. Red and blue carpets lie ready at hand, and on these carpets Prince Ahmad will enter the City of Happiness . . .'

'And I am creeping around here in the rocks like a snake!' cried the lad.

'My advice to you,' said the wood-merchant, 'is to remain hidden. In Bagdad Djaffah's horsemen will lay hold of you.'

'Oh,' cried Ali, 'I shall go down all the same! Up there, by the tamarisks, I have a bundle filled with blue silk and yellow cloth. If I put that on no one will recognize me. I must go to see Ahmad the Prince, riding through the gates into the City of Happiness! Also, the ambassador of the Shah-in-shah will protect me.'

'Oh, of course!' laughed Ali Baba. 'This venerable Whitebeard is only just waiting for a beggar-boy to turn up!' (If you only knew, thought the lad, if you only knew, bandy-legged Ali Baba!) But aloud he said: 'First I have got to find a Sufi who lives somewhere round here in a cave.'

'Is this Sufi's name Baba, perhaps, like mine—just Baba?' inquired the wood-merchant.

'Yes,' agreed Ali, 'that's his name!'

Ali Baba pointed with his arm and said: 'Go up there, where my donkeys have stopped, then turn left. You will find a cleft in the rocks—very narrow. After a hundred paces it broadens out. Follow it but pay attention to your feet; it swarms with snakes. Sand-vipers and that sort of thing! One bite and you are finished for all time. Well, the ravine leads for half an hour deep into the mountains. There you will find the Sufi. It may be he will say a word to you. To me he has never said anything although I have often met him.'

'Allah send you much dried wood, Ali Baba!' said the boy. 'Now I can find the way!'

Ali Baba raised his eyebrows and scratched his red

beard. 'Take care what you say, little friend. This Sufi is a holy man! At night he receives visitors in his cave—ghosts and such like! Sometimes even the angel Gabriel comes to see him. Then they discuss things together, like Muhammad the Prophet, who, in his time, talked with the angel Gabriel.'

Almost speechless with awe, Ali said: 'He must indeed be a very holy man.'

Then Ali Baba asked: 'Have you been long up here in the woods?'

Ali made a gesture embracing the glowing rocks to the east and the escarpment in the west, over the rim of which could be seen the ruddy mist covering the plain.

'Since sunrise!' he said, and added: 'I could not find any water and am thirsty from eating dry food.'

Ali Baba handed the boy his water-flask and, with a look of cunning, asked: 'Haven't you seen anything—I mean—people?'

'Ah!' Ali smacked his lips. 'That was marvellous!' He returned the flask and licked up a remaining drop of water. 'You mean . . .?'

'Yes, yes,' said Ali Baba, his fingers twirling his red beard.

'Oh yes!' Ali nodded. 'I saw some men, just before midday. They were on foot and went over the side there, in the west.'

'How many?' asked the wood-merchant excitedly.

'I counted thirty-nine, then after a while another came along.'

'That makes forty altogether!' gasped Ali Baba. 'Forty thieves that makes!'

'Yes, and they went westwards, down the mountain,' said Ali.

'The hour is favourable!' chuckled Ali Baba. 'I must go; I know where these fellows live! Farewell, little friend!' He stepped over a boulder and hobbled on his bandy legs after his donkeys.

Ali grinned and turned towards the rocks. It was not long before he found the cleft on the left-hand side and after half an hour's careful walking, discovered the holy man's cave at the end of the ravine.

At that moment the Sufi was standing at the entrance of his underground home. He wore the thick woollen garment of all Sufis, woven from pale camel's hair, girded with a coarse cord. He stood in the sand with folded arms whilst at his bare feet a viper moved, a yellow creature as long as a man's arm, carrying swift and terrible death in its jaws.

Frightened, Ali held his breath. The snake took itself off amongst the stones. He raised his head and looked straight into the face of the Sufi, a haggard face, burnt brown, with two narrow, coal-black eyes. Then he noticed for the first time that these eyes were steadily fixed on him. He made a deep obeisance, his forehead touching the stones and said:

'Peace be with you, O Brother of the Present!'

It was thus the Sufis called themselves from the very beginning.

A smile hovered on the hermit's thin lips.

'I have been sent by Asoka to you—' said Ali '—Asoka, a venerable nobleman from Hindustan.'

The Sufi inclined his head slightly. Encouraged, Ali went on: 'His beard is as white as silver in the sun; his eyes —holy brother—his eyes never blink when he looks at you.'

The black eyes of the Sufi regarded him steadily. Ali lowered his eyelids and began to dig with his big toe in the sand. He could hear his own heart beating, the only sound in this shadowy hollow.

'Speak, little brother!'

Ali gave a start. The Sufi's words had awakened an echo amongst the rocks. All at once he recollected why he had come here.

'It's a question—' he got out with difficulty '—of a magic lamp. I am looking for it because it can fulfil every wish——'

The Sufi inclined his head.

'I have asked everyone about it: story-tellers, water-carriers—even the great and wise Abu Bekr, a very learned man in all arts and sciences; Sindbad the sailor, who has travelled far; I asked him as well. Abu Bekr, alone, gave me some information. He said the magic lamp was hidden on the island of Qalah. I went there in Sind-bad's ship, but there isn't any island of Qalah——'

'Speak on!' said the Sufi.

'—and now, what must I do to find it? Do you know anything about it? It is a very wonderful lamp; it fulfils every wish. It used to belong to Aladdin.' Ali glanced nervously at the tight lips.

Then the Sufi said: 'You have been searching far and wide. Too far! You have spoken to many. Too many! Close your eyes!'

Ali pressed his lids together. He felt his left knee trembling and expected some witchcraft. Instead there sounded only the soft but rich voice of the Sufi with the question:

'What can you see?'

'Nothing,' answered Ali.

'Now stop your ears for a moment!' commanded the Sufi.

Ali obeyed, laying the palms of his hands against his ears and then taking them away.

The Sufi asked: 'What did you hear?'

'Nothing,' answered Ali.

'Now, little brother,' said the hermit, 'with these eyes and with these ears you have been looking for a miracle—the lamp which fulfils every wish?'

Ali noticed the gentle smile. He thought for a moment he had understood what lay behind this question; but the meaning escaped and vanished. In a small voice he said:

'I don't know . . .'

'Now you have made the first step towards wonderful things, little brother!' said the Sufi. 'You have just said "I don't know". That is the first step. The second is called Knowledge.'

'What must I know?' asked Ali, confused.

'Al Haqq!' replied the Sufi.

'What is that?' asked Ali.

'It is that which always remains the same. It is that which is unchanging, that which is not, grows not and does not pass away.'

Ali shook his head sadly.

Then the Sufi asked: 'Can you see with closed eyes?'

'No,' said Ali.

'Can you hear with stopped ears?'

'No,' said Ali.

'And further,' continued the Sufi, 'things heard and things seen—do these two remain or do they finally pass away?'

'Things seen disappear,' said Ali. 'Things heard also—you forget them.'

The Sufi inclined his head and said with a smile:

'Well, little brother, you must understand that the lamp is old and inconspicuous. Its shape is well-known; a lamp like other lamps! You could break it with your hands; it is made of the same material as all the lamps in Saoud:

176

copper, brass or clay. Shape and material are unimportant. Important, however, is the flame that burns in its mouth. The name of this flame is—Al Haqq. It is Al Haqq that you must find!'

That word again, thought Ali, making a long face. This Sufi recommended Al Haqq; Abu Bekr had recommended Qalah—he shook his head and, overcome with a sudden doubt, said:

'Is it true, holy brother, that you talk at night with the angel Gabriel, as Muhammad used to do?'

'No!' answered the Sufi, amused.

'Perhaps even the Prophet never spoke to the angel!' said Ali bitterly. All seemed lost. This Sufi Baba knew no more than anybody else!

'It is quite possible that Muhammad saw the angel Gabriel,' the hermit then said. 'Perhaps Muhammad even spoke with him. Whether he understood him though, that is as great a question as whether you have understood my words, little brother.'

Ali slowly shook his head and said: 'No, holy one, I did not understand your words. All the same—accept my thanks! Only tell me just this: what does Al Haqq mean? Then I will go.'

'Al Haqq,' answered the Sufi, 'means Reality! Never forget, little brother, only the true and loyal will ever find a miracle! Only when your heart is pure and honest will a miracle take place. When you are merely using your eyes and your ears, you will only be holding an ordinary lamp in your hands.'

Ali listened with bowed head. When he again looked up, the low entrance to the cave yawned dark and empty: the Sufi had vanished.

He wandered back through the ravine, feeling tired and

bitterly disappointed. By the time he had reached the narrow cleft leading down the slope, a blood-red disc hung over the black, gnarled trees—the sun was sinking. He scrambled on down through thickets and sped towards the City of Happiness.

It was midnight when he crossed the river; not by the bridge of boats, but swimming with a bundle tied round his neck. Nobody noticed the small head bobbing in the water under the stars.

He slipped through the streets and alleys swiftly and noiselessly, like a bad conscience; pushed the tattered carpet aside and crept into the old beggar-woman's hovel. He listened, sniffed the musty air, and felt his way to the bed of rags in the corner.

As he unwrapped his wet loin-cloth, a sigh reached his ear. The old woman lay awake in the darkness. Then he heard her voice, faint, almost chuckling as she said:

'You are back—you weren't drowned in the Tigris?'

Ali listened and thought: perhaps she thinks I'm a ghost. He answered: 'No, here I am. I wasn't drowned.'

Whispering in the darkness, the old woman said: 'You must leave here before daybreak, grandson. They could find you here . . .'

'They have other things to do!' said Ali. 'Bagdad is expecting Ahmad of Hindustan. Tomorrow I shall go to the Caliph's court; nothing will happen to me. And now—' he added, '—now I must sleep.' Hunger gnawed at his inside but his drowsiness was the stronger.

He fell at once into a deep, dreamless sleep.

When he opened his eyes the holes in the old curtain shone bright. He stared for a moment in front of him, then collected his thoughts and remembered who he was: Ali, the beggar, who had once been a thief and a cabin-boy and who was now in the pay of an ambassador from Hindustan; Ali, who was still searching for the magic lamp . . .

Words ran through his head—words which the holy man had spoken yesterday in the mountains. He threw off the threadbare blanket and raised himself on the rags.

'A lamp like other lamps . . .'

He stood up. In the half-light of the musty cave he went to the low table that stood by the old woman's bed.

'. . . made of the same material as all the lamps in Saoud . . .' the Sufi had said.

He took hold of the old lamp which stood on the little table. It was a dinted and dirty thing, made of copper; something that belonged to Ali's memory as much as his two feet. As far back as he could recollect, this lamp had always been there. Night after night a sooty flame had flickered in the bent mouth, fed with oil begged at the Gate of the Prophet.

Ali weighed the thing thoughtfully in his right hand.

A few moments later the bent old beggar-woman came in from the street. In a corner of her dress she carried a flat loaf. She found Ali kneeling on the bare floor. The lamp was burning; the reflection flickered in his big eyes.

A fool, thought the old woman. I had a feeling that he was mad! Crouching there and wasting oil in broad daylight! The toothless mouth opened and then snapped to as the lad asked:

'Where did you get this lamp from?'

She gave a chuckle. Mad! Obviously a fool! And she began to mutter under her breath a rambling spell, an exhortation that was used in those days in Saoud against harm and evil spirits whenever anyone was found to be mad. Then she said:

'Your mother brought this lamp with her from Basra

179

when she carried you, my poor foolish grandson, to the City of Happiness. She died, my good daughter, and left you with me—you—the gift of a sailor—you—just a fool! Oh my poor grandson!'

The jaws closed.

'Oh . . .' said Ali very slowly.

The flame was now burning steadily in the copper mouth. The smell of burnt oil penetrated his nose; but he did not notice it. ' . . . only when you are loyal and true . . .' the Sufi had said, ' . . . only then will a miracle happen.'

He closed his eyes and thought: Am I honest and true?

The beggar-woman hobbled around behind his back and began again with her spell. Without any doubt her grandson was possessed by an evil spirit, invisible and mischievous, which had crept under his skin! Her withered lips formed the words of the exhortation as well as she could remember them. At last she paused for breath, but the boy took no notice of her.

He was thinking of the beautiful little maid in the garden of the Caliph. To her he had promised the magic lamp. Should this lamp between his knees, should it be the magic lamp, then it belonged to the maiden with the big, dark eyes. In that case he must take it to her, whether he would or no. He had promised it her. It is true she had taken him for a Djinn; but he knew only too well that this mistake could make no difference. Either, so he thought, I am honest: in which case this will become Aladdin's magic lamp, and then I must give it to her! Or, if I keep it, then I am dishonest and the lamp will remain what it has always been: just an ordinary dented copper lamp.

Slowly he opened his eyes. The small flame blinded him. Thin, golden rays of light streamed from the mouth of the copper lamp. Then he suddenly remembered the word. It was the name of this flame, burning before him and dazzling his eyes. He said loudly and clearly:

'Al Haqq!'

The beggar-woman leaned back against the wall, frightened.

He got up from the floor and seized his bundle of clothes. His dirty, red loin-cloth fell to the ground. From the yellow cloth he wound himself trousers, such as he had seen the merchants who came from Hindustan wearing. He carefully combed out his hair and bound the blue silk in a turban round his head, beautiful and neat, such as only men who came from Hindustan wore.

None of Djaffah's horsemen would now recognize him!

He gave a laugh, loud and happy; and once more the old woman cringed away from him. He paid no attention.

Soon now he would be seeing Whitebeard from Hindustan and hear his melodious voice!

Soon now would he see Ahmad of Hindustan—who was to enter, over costly carpets, the gates of the City of Happiness!

He bent down, picked up the lamp in his right hand and turned towards the doorway. With his left, he grasped the dirty curtain and pulled it aside. Bright daylight struck his forehead. The beggar-woman gave a loud and hoarse cry and covered her face with her hands. Her eyes were blinded: a lustre, a brilliance, a radiant light had she seen on the lad's brow, just as though a magic gem had shone through the skin of his forehead.

Here and there the head of a horse bearing a black-draped rider appeared above the dense throng of people; Djaffah's soldiers were everywhere to be seen, at every corner of the bazaars, for the news of the immediate arrival of the Indian prince had brought untold numbers from the countryside into the city. But not one of these guards recognized Ali, the beggar. What momentarily met their eyes was a brown youth in a blue silk turban.

In the middle of the bridge stood Hassan, the potter's offspring, surrounded by his rough companions. The tall fellow gaped stupidly at the dinted copper lamp, carried in a boy's hand.

On the other side of the river Ali Baba, the wood-merchant, was riding on a load of sticks; underneath the load trotted a grey donkey with thin legs and, behind, followed his mates, bobbing their heads. The lad grinned as the red beard up aloft approached; he winked with his left eye and made a face. The good Ali Baba looked down but noticed nothing.

But now—Allah!—the walls, bathed in the light of the climbing sun, dazzled him; the white walls, the Palace of the Caliph!

The gate stood wide open, for Haroun al-Raschid was expecting the Prince of Hindustan!

Horsemen on chargers, their green mantles billowing round them; deep red turbans and sparkling sabre-blades; he took no heed of them. He slipped out of the gaping crowd, forcing his way through sweating bodies, and stepped lightly up to the guards whose horses were pawing at the dust.

Both hands encircled the old lamp.

And as in those days when there had been nothing but sunshine and blue sky; just as in those days on Sindbad's lovely ship, he forgot himself and was no longer aware whether he was Ali the thief, Ali the beggar, Ali the cabin-boy, or perhaps none of these. In this moment he was just

a boy whose heart beat—beat for very joy. All that his eyes
had ever seen was forgotten. All the names he had ever
borne were forgotten. With wide-open eyes he had come
to see a marvel; a Prince of Hindustan who was entering
the City of Happiness! A Spirit which emerged from a
copper lamp! And his ears were ready for new names . . .

The black chargers reared and backed away from his
path. Their riders tried to bar his way with sword and
lance but could not reach him.

He went through the open gate, carrying the lamp in his
hands.

The courtyard was broad and extensive; light glittered
from the coloured flag-stones. From left and right soldiers

disengaged from the shadows of the walls, like the swarms of birds on the island of Mullak; they tried to stop the youth from entering the palace, shouting and waving their arms about as they ran.

At that very moment a man stepped out from under the shady columns and arches at the farthest end of the courtyard. Trumpet-calls resounded in the air; there was a rattle as the soldiers threw themselves on the ground with bowed heads.

But the man beckoned to the boy with both his hands.

And he ran forward, the old lamp pressed tightly against his breast.

That man was Haroun al-Raschid, the Caliph. And behind him came out of the shade into the sunshine—a white flowing beard.

'Most worthy one!' panted the lad. 'There—here it is'— He sank down on his knees on a red paving-stone and with both hands held out the little dinted lamp to Whitebeard. 'Take it; look at it, Worthy One. The magic lamp!'

The old man smiled.

The Caliph approached them and bent down.

Then the boy said: 'Lord! This is the magic lamp out of the legend. It fulfils every wish if you rub it with your hand, but it does not belong to me! It belongs to a young girl, brown and sweet, who was in your garden by the Tigris three days ago—a girl in yellow silk!'

'That girl,' said Haroun al-Raschid, 'is the Princess of Peshawar. A Djinn promised her Aladdin's lamp.'

'Yes, yes,' said the boy, embarrassed, 'that was a lie. It wasn't a Djinn——'

'The Princess of Peshawar has been waiting for you since that very hour!' said the Caliph, clasping his hands. 'Arise, royal friend of my eyes!'

The lad got up and started back.

Now the whitebearded old man crossed his arms and, bowing his head, said in his strong, deep voice:

'Greeting, at last, Ahmad, Prince of Hindustan!'

The copper lamp fell and rolled at his feet as the lad laid his hands on his bare chest and stammered:

'I—I am——'

'Oh yes!' said Whitebeard. His big eyes shone. 'Oh yes, you are he! That is why we travelled from land to land! For you!'

'For me?'

'For none other, son of my old days!' said smilingly the Whitebeard from Hindustan.

Four hooves clattered over the flag-stones. Nearby a white arab was reined in. A lean rider jumped from the saddle, threw himself on his knees before the brown youth and cried:

'Do you recognize your servant, Prince? I am Sar, the horseman, out of Djaffah's dungeon under the earth.'

'Allah!' said the boy. 'You!' He looked into the dark eyes under the white turban.

'Give the order for us to ride!' said the young man. 'Rama Muni is approaching from the east over the mountains with his hirelings. Your father has placed his hopes in you, Prince Ahmad.'

'My father?' The boy slowly shook his head and said: 'My father was a sailor.'

'Oh no, Prince!' answered Whitebeard. 'That sailor only brought you from Hindustan to Basra. He gave you to a stranger woman because he had no wish to kill you, as Rama Muni wanted, after he had stolen you.'

'Stolen me?'

'Already on the rocky desert island of Mullak I

recognized you, Prince Ahmad,' said Whitebeard. 'You did not look like a cabin-boy, much more like a prince who knew nothing of his father's kingdom and thought he was a beggar. I put you to the proof. Now that is all finished. Today the whole world shall hear that you are Ahmad, our Lord and Prince of Hindustan!'

'Hindustan!' said the brown-skinned lad, dropping his head. 'When I first heard that word, Hindustan, it was as if—I don't know——'

'Give the command for us to ride, Prince Ahmad!' pressed Sar, still on his knees on the paving-stones.

'Come into the shade, my Prince and friend,' said Haroun al-Raschid. 'It is nearly midday. A hundred fans of ostrich-feathers will relieve you from the heat. A cooling drink, fruit and sweet delicacies are prepared for you. And the Princess of Peshawar is waiting for you . . .'

'This Rama Muni,' said the boy, turning to Whitebeard, 'this disloyal Grand Vizier really stole me when I was an innocent baby?'

'It is so!' said the old man.

'He wanted to kill me?'

'He did!' nodded the Whitebeard.

'And because of him I do not know my father nor my native land, have lived as a beggar, have hungered in rags?'

'Because of him!' answered the old man. 'He wanted to seize power. He still wants that.'

'And now he is crossing the mountains from the east and intends to attack my father's kingdom with his hired Mongols. Is all that true?'

'Most assuredly, Prince Ahmad!' cried Sar, springing to his feet. 'There is need for great haste, O Prince.'

Then the brown, half-naked youth drew himself up to his full height. His eyes flashed in the sunlight; he threw up his head and cried so that it could be heard over the broad courtyard and over the soldiers' heads:

'I appeal to all loyal men in Saoud who have waited for this day! Saddle the horses! In the name of Allah follow me to Hindustan!'

Thereupon Sar shouted for joy and the soldiers brandished their weapons and shouted with him. The white-bearded old man smiled and bowed. With a sweep of his arm the Caliph invited the Prince of Hindustan into his palace. But before they had even taken a step, the stone courtyard resounded to the hooves of the white arab, which swept out through the gateway. And Ahmad, who but an hour ago had been called Ali, said:

'If there are only a thousand young men in my father's kingdom like this horseman Sar, then Rama Muni and his yellow hordes are lost.' Only then did he follow the Caliph into the cool, shady halls of the palace to partake, sitting on soft cushions, of food and drink.

It was the hour of midday.

And the streets and bazaars of the City of Happiness echoed with the rejoicings of the people. With ten thousand open mouths Bagdad shouted its joy: for the Caliph's heralds had everywhere proclaimed the arrival of Prince Ahmad.

Yet once again, fourteen days later, the gay crowds in this city gave him an ovation, accompanying him to the eastern gate where, surrounded by his followers, he rode across the Tigris. In Bagdad he had been a beggar. Now this city roared his name and his future glory out into the sunshine.

Beggar—he thought as he rode through the tumult—first a beggar and now a prince. Life is a funny thing!

Yet his heart was sad as he reined his horse under the

187

shadow of the archway. Someone was left behind. And that person was none other than that old beggar-woman who, since the day of his glory, had disappeared and could not be found. She had fed him and given him shelter, year after year. He had been Ali, the thief; Ali, the beggar-boy. Now that he had become Ahmad, Prince of Hindustan, he had lost her!

To himself, however, he swore:

In my kingdom the old shall be honoured! Is it not due to them that I am here today? The Whitebeard brought me the inheritance of a far-off kingdom. The old beggar-woman kept me until this time. And, he thought further, there may be other princes being looked after in their poverty by beggar-women, other heirs of unbeknown kingdoms waiting for their Whitebeard. That shall not be forgotten!

He gently spurred his white arab and rode the length of the column of men until he came to a camel, attended by black servants, and bearing a swaying tent of blue silk on its back. Here he leant over from the saddle and parted the fluttering curtains with his hand.

'Little friend, light of my eyes!' he cried. 'The mountains are near. Give me the magic lamp unless you wish to keep it!'

'I do not want to keep it!' answered the lovely maiden in the blue tent, and she laughed gaily. 'What do I want with a magic lamp? Is it not wonderful enough that a beggar has been turned into a Djinn, into a prince, in fact?'

'You could fulfil every wish!' warned the young prince, riding very close beside the patient camel. 'Rub it hard with your hand, little friend, wish for fortune or happiness; what you will!'

The laughing reply came out of the folds of blue silk:

188

'What do I want with riches? I, the Princess of Peshawar?'

'What indeed, little friend!' cried young Prince Ahmad. 'You, the Princess of Hindustan!' He withdrew his hand, his fingers closed round the old, dirty, dinted copper lamp. Then he turned his arab round and dashed off across the road towards the red mountains.

The sun was already sinking in the west as he tied his white stallion to a twisted tamarisk-tree and entered the narrow cleft in the rocks. On foot and alone, as once before, he walked calmly along the ravine, ignoring the snakes, until he came to the lonely cave in the hollow where the Sufi lived.

'What are you bringing, little brother?' asked the holy man.

'Thirty-four days ago,' said the brown lad, bowing so low that his white silk turban brushed the ground, 'I came to you, holy brother, and my name was Ali, the beggar. I asked you about the wonderful lamp. I have found it and so have returned; but I am now called Ahmad, Prince of Hindustan. Here is the lamp, O Brother of the Present. Keep it for all time, so that it may be found by you, O Friend of the Faithful, should anyone again seek this marvel.'

'Little brother,' answered the Sufi in a friendly voice, taking the old lamp in his hands, 'there will always be young beggars and young princes asking for this wonder. And they shall find it if they are loyal and honest in their hearts.'

Night had fallen when he untied the snorting stallion from the tamarisk. He led the animal by the bridle over the dark crevices along the rugged mountain ridge. Towards midnight he could see the camp-fires, like little red stars, down below in the valley. He then swung himself into the saddle, giving his horse free rein; and as the full moon rose over the ancient land of Saoud and over the ancient River Tigris, he rode past the guard into the camp.

'Allah!' he said, tired but grateful. 'These sleeping men are my friends.'

'Allah,' said the old man from Hindustan, his beard flowing like silver in the moonlight. Seizing the hanging reins, he added in his ringing voice: '*He* alone is the one true friend.'

It is another story how Ahmad, who used to be known as Ali, rode through the rocky mountain passes, where the horses nearly died of thirst; how he, in his snow-white turban, and mounted on his white arab, carried the green silk flag into the plain and on into Hindustan; how he, amidst a whirlwind of trampling horses, clashing swords, whistling arrows, swept back the mercenaries of Rama Muni; how he struck off the head of the traitorous Grand Vizier; and how he sank on his knees before his white-bearded father and kissed his hands. And so at last he came home.

ALLAH is the Arabic name for God; whoever believes in Him is known either as a Muslim or a Muhammedan; for Muhammad was Allah's Prophet. A Muslim (or Moslem) does not go to church but prays in a mosque. From the tower of the mosque, known as a minaret, is cried out the *muezzin*, or call to prayer.

In Ali's time the Faithful were ruled by the Caliph, who lived in Bagdad on the River Tigris. One of these Caliphs, Haroun al-Raschid, has been made famous through the *Arabian Nights* stories. A Vizier, in those days, was a kind of Prime Minister; a Shah was a sovereign ruler; and the Shah-in-shah was the King over the other sovereign rulers in a land.

The cloth bound round the head is known as a turban; a broad cloak with a hood, a burnous. A caftan is a long under-tunic, and a haik an outer wrapper not unlike a burnous. Warriors carried in their girdles a scimitar, a dangerous curved kind of sword. The bazaars were, and still are, open markets where one bought what was needed, paying for it with dirhams or dinars—Arabian money.

In the *Koran*, the sacred writings of the Arabs, there is talk of Shaitan, the devil. However, a proper Sufi does not believe in him, for he is a free-thinking hermit who, in silent prayer, contemplates only the name of Allah. Ordinary folk, on the other hand, believe in Shaitan, just as they believe in ghouls and djinns; that is to say in goblins and evil spirits.

If you wanted to be polite to your neighbour you greeted him with the words: '*Salaam oleikum*', which in our language means, 'Peace be with you'.

The four lines of poetry on page 57 come from an old Arabian poet; but I have forgotten his name.